PENELOPE MARCH is MELTING

PENELOPE MARCH is MELTING

JEFFREY MICHAEL RUBY

DELACORTE PRESS

Text copyright © 2017 by Jeffrey Michael Ruby
Jacket art copyright © 2017 by Alexandria Neonakis

randomhousekids.com

Educators and librarians, for a variety of teaching tools, visit us at RHTeachersLibrarians.com

Library of Congress Cataloging-in-Publication Data
Names: Ruby, Jeff, author.
Title: Penelope March is melting / Jeff Ruby.
Description: First edition. | New York: Delacorte Press, [2017] |
Summary: Twelve-year-old bookworm Penelope becomes an unlikely hero when the iceberg she calls home starts to melt, and she must save it from a sinister force.
Identifiers: LCCN 2016031613 | ISBN 978-1-5247-1828-2 (hc) |
ISBN 978-1-5247-1830-5 (ebook)
Subjects: | CYAC: Icebergs—Fiction. | Family life—Fiction. | Heroes—Fiction.
Classification: LCC PZ7.1.R8277 Pen 2017 | DDC [Fic]—dc23

The text of this book is set in 13-point Kennedy Book.

Printed in the United States of America
10 9 8 7 6 5 4 3 2 1
First Edition

TO MOM, WHO LED THE WAY AND
WHO NEVER GIVES UP

CHAPTER 1

Years ago, scientists spotted a strange iceberg float-ing a hundred miles off the coast of Antarctica. That part of the world is full of icebergs, so one off by itself in the middle of nowhere isn't so odd. The odd part is what the scientists found when they studied satellite images of the iceberg.

It was hard to tell from the grainy photos, but there appeared to be people living on the iceberg. A whole town, with roads and cars and houses. A school and a church. One image seemed to show a man walk-ing a dog.

Three countries—the United States, Argentina, and Japan—sent explorers in small planes to the coordinates where the iceberg had been spotted.

All three found nothing. The American and Argentinean planes returned with no answers; the Japanese plane never returned. Whether the iceberg had continued to float farther out into the ocean, or sunk, or melted, no one knew. But it was gone. As disappointed as they were, the scientists moved on to projects more sensible than looking for populated icebergs.

Penelope March woke up in her hammock with her lips stuck to page 287.

Most mornings, she opened her eyes to find a book over her face or tucked in her arm or under her head and serving as a terribly ineffective pillow. But on this particular morning she had to separate her dry mouth from the page. Painful as it was, far worse was the notion that she had only fifty-one pages left and would have to finish it later.

Penelope was twelve years old and loved books. Magazines. Signs. Instructional manuals. Anything with words, really. Her fingers often grabbed whatever was closest without her telling them to, like the time at the doctor when her hands got so itchy she spent an hour reading a pamphlet about the dangers of pancreatitis.

But Penelope especially gravitated toward books that included a "plucky heroine," a brassy and clever girl who saved the day using nothing but her wits and cunning. She was currently reading *The Impossible Glories and Misfortunes of Nicola Torland,* M. Winston McCann's thick and unforgiving book about an orphan who woke up with one of her ears missing and spent the next twenty-eight chapters figuring out who, why, and how. By the end of part one, Nicola Torland had become a double agent, a world-class archer, and the most respected philosopher in her country. And she was only fourteen. And had one ear.

Penelope examined her reflection in the bathroom mirror. She had two healthy ears and she had not yet become much of anything. She'd studied her own face so many times—the big eyes, the rowdy mop of hair, the chin so wide the freckles on one side did not seem to know about the freckles on the other—that she could no longer tell if she was pretty or hideous or somewhere in between. And she had tried desperately to stop caring.

She gave up and opened the medicine chest in search of toothpaste. Taped to the toothpaste inside the medicine chest was a note in blocky handwriting:

*What word becomes shorter when
you add two letters to it?*

Penelope smiled. *Oh, Miles.*

Her little brother had been leaving riddles and
jokes for her lately. Penelope and Miles shared a
room in a tiny house on Broken Branch Lane, a drab
street tucked into a valley on the south side of Glacier Cove. Their room had two hammocks, a desk, a
little window, and not much space to maneuver. Privacy was out of the question.

Even on their modest block, neighbors whispered
about the poor state of the family's house, a ramshackle structure that appeared to be held together
by little more than spit, tape, and luck. On unpleasant days, it waved and buckled like drapes in the
wind. "That *shack*," sneered their next-door neighbor,
Mrs. Shaw, to her husband. "I thought last night's
storm would send it flying away, with the three of
them inside it."

Though the house embarrassed their father to
no end, Penelope and Miles gave no indication that
it bothered them. They had never known anything
different. Both were simply grateful for the roof over
their heads.

Glacier Cove did not qualify as a wealthy town, but some inhabitants certainly had more than others. The lucky ones dressed in nicer clothes, ate better food, lived in larger homes. However, even the lucky ones had to admit that Glacier Cove did not live up to its promising name. Sure, there was the Ice Lantern Festival in December, when every citizen over the age of six lit their own homemade orb, charging the sky with a rich orange glow that lasted for ten glorious minutes if it wasn't a windy night. And every other February, there were the Deep-Freeze Games, a grand extravaganza of athletic competitions.

But the town was cold and dreary, and the snow that fell was not a peaceful, soft white but rather was rough and gray. If a child was foolish enough to try catching a snowflake on his tongue, he usually got an ice pebble in the eye. If you fell asleep with a runny nose, which was pretty much always, you woke up with a boogersicle. As you can imagine, dealing with a boogersicle that's been forming on your face for nine hours is not an ideal way to start your day. Most people prefer breakfast.

In Glacier Cove, that breakfast usually included turnips, which grew in abundance, regardless of the season. How could a place so miserably cold, where the ground had been covered with thick layers of ice for as long as anyone could recall, produce so many turnips, which only grow in warm climates? The truth was, no one knew, and no one questioned it. Local scientists had taken advantage of the oddity and developed ways to use turnips to produce both gasoline and electricity. This was perhaps the town's greatest miracle, unless you count the time the Funkhauser twins got frozen inside their chimney for six hours and only broke free by peeing on each other.

But Glacier Cove had floated alone in the middle of the ocean for as long as anyone could remember. In spite of the people's ingenuity, they had a blind spot when it came to exploration. If there was a larger world out there, they certainly didn't wish to brave the icy waters to find out.

Instead, they ate their turnips and wore their coats outdoors and indoors. For twenty-three hours and fifty-nine minutes a day, they bundled up in gloves and hats, shivering and sniffling.

The other minute was even worse, because that was when the people of Glacier Cove showered. During that dreadful sixty seconds, off came layer upon layer of clothes, which smelled like a mix of dried sweat and rotting turnips. The typical Glacier Covian would turn on the shower, which spat out thick blasts of freezing water, and he would jump around and shriek like a blind baboon while he fumbled for the soap, which also smelled like turnips, to rub against various unpleasant parts of his pasty skin that ended up splotchy and irritated, angry at even a minute of exposure to the brutal air.

You don't want to know about their baths.

After a frosty shower, Penelope walked into the kitchen with *Nicola Torland* tucked under her arm. She found her brother and father eating identical breakfasts: a bowl of Turnip Flakes, a glass of turnip juice, and a turnip. They had set the same breakfast for her.

"So, today's riddle," Miles said over the scrape and ding of spoon to bowl. "What word becomes shorter when you add two letters to it?"

Penelope knew it was a trick question, like all Miles's riddles were. But the more she thought about it—*Shorter? How was that even possible?*—the more her head hurt.

"Pen, Pen, Pen," Miles chided through a goofy grin that could not be stopped by the heaps of cereal he was shoveling into his mouth. "I'm disappointed in you." He glanced at Penelope's book. "Did you know M. Winston McCann wrote naked? Every day, he took off his clothes and gave them to his wife. Then he locked himself in his room to write."

"Why?"

"To keep himself from going to the pub."

"Eat your breakfast," mumbled their father, a large man with bloodshot eyes and a hurricane of a beard. He'd grown accustomed to their inside jokes, though he usually found himself on the outside. "You're going to be late for school."

"Come on, Miles!"

They tramped through the snow on Silver Sky Road, Penelope's younger brother a good ten paces behind her. All elbows and ears, Miles tried to work himself out of a pair of handcuffs he'd found behind the police station last week. He had wriggled the handcuffs over his head with his double-jointed arms, but his bulky gloves certainly didn't help. "Hey, wait for me!" he called. "Look! I've almost got it."

Though a year younger than Penelope, Miles stood roughly the same height. Old ladies constantly mistook them for twins. But he and his sister were very different.

Miles liked books just fine; he just happened to prefer people. And people liked Miles, because he was always himself, and that self was happy. You know how newborn babies enter the world crying? Baby Miles did not cry. He slid out, wet and wild, rubbed his eyes, and glanced around the delivery room as if searching for answers. Finding none, he broke into what would be called a toothy smile if he'd had any teeth. It wasn't until a nurse cut the umbilical cord that Miles began wailing, and that seemed more out of confusion. *Hey, isn't that part of my body you're throwing away there?* When he realized he didn't need the cord after all, his grin returned.

On Silver Sky Road, even after wincing at the grotesque snap of his shoulder—which Miles had popped out of its socket so he could pick the hand-cuff lock with a paper clip—he smiled. He fumbled for a moment; then, *click,* the cuffs slipped into the snow at his feet.

As he reached down, though, Miles's smile faded.

His body froze as his eyes locked on something in the distance.

"Miles? Are you okay?"

Penelope followed her brother's gaze across Silver Sky Road, past a bleak expanse of dirty slush, and the daily stab of fear nicked her chest.

The Ice House.

The kids had heard all the stories. The Ice House—a big, creepy mansion with an ice roof, ice walls, an ice door, ice windows, an ice driveway, and an ice porch with a swing forever frozen in place—had been built by a black-toothed vampire who slept in an igloo in the basement, guarded by a dog named Wolfknuckle that barked like a foghorn and bit like a tiger. If that wasn't scary enough, a pair of testy ice gargoyles scowled from the roof at anyone who dared catch their hollow eyes. The only thing that moved was a giant clock over the front door, *tick-tick-tick*ing to mark the minutes you had left should you dare to enter.

Some said the house's halls were decorated not with furniture but with *children*. The foolish ones who had ventured inside, usually on a dare, had immediately turned to ice, their faces frozen forever in shock and fear at whatever horrible thing they had seen in their last moment.

All anyone knew for certain was that a strange old man named Buzzardstock lived there and that he had thin green hair and a mole on his nose with so much hair of its own that it looked like a small broccoli. On this particular morning, the thought of Buzzardstock's broccoli mole was enough to convince Penelope to avoid the Ice House.

Miles bent to pick up the handcuffs, slow and quiet, so as not to risk disturbing Wolfknuckle. He bit his lip and popped his rubbery shoulder back into its socket.

"Let's go," said Penelope, grabbing her brother's hand.

The siblings ran all the way to school, their boots squeaking in the fresh snow. On the way, Penelope noticed a small crack in the ice that perpetually covered Archibald Fountain in front of city hall, but she gave it no thought. She and Miles arrived sweaty and gasping for breath, just two more noisy children dashing up the school steps two at a time to make it to first period.

The bell rang, teachers tapped their chalkboards

until things quieted down, and another day at Glacier Cove Academy began.

The whole school might not have been so carefree had they known that right beneath them, something terrible was happening. And if they continued with their lives as they were, they would all be dead within the year.

CHAPTER 2

"Who can tell me—*HIC*—how many amendments there are in the—*HIC*—Glacier Cove—*HICKHUCKHURP*—oh, Lord, sorry! . . . erm, in the Glacier Cove Constitution?"

Penelope's sixth-grade teacher, Mr. Stingleberry, had suffered from the hiccups since he was a teenager. On top of that, he had a noticeable limp that seemed to get worse when he was hiccupping, which was always. He wasn't such a bad teacher, just a simpleminded one, and his job always seemed to get in the way of his one true goal in life: getting rid of the hiccups.

Rather than answer their teacher's question, the amused children offered suggestions for curing the hiccups, which started out intended to help and only got more ridiculous.

"You should drink a glass of water."

"Have you tried standing on your head?"

"My mom says plugging your ears—"

"Try taking off your underwear and putting it on backwards."

Stingleberry waved off every suggestion. He had heard and tried it all with no success. He knew from experience that the old underwear trick most certainly did *not* work, and if you've ever put your underwear on backward, you know it's pretty uncomfortable, which for poor Mr. Stingleberry meant that he had not only the hiccups but also an atrocious wedgie of his own making.

Without warning, the hiccups disappeared. Pleased, Stingleberry limped to the chalkboard. "Now, the number of amendments in the Glacier Cove Constitution . . . Anyone?" He took a gulp of turnip soda and waited. He sighed. These kids. "The Glacier Cove Constitution currently has . . . *HIC!*"

The kids exploded into laughter so hysterical that Principal Flincher—a shrill woman shaped like a bowling pin and with a personality to match— burst into the classroom in her polka-dotted parka and told them to hush for Pete's sake and stop mocking this poor man's problem. They hushed just long enough for Mrs. Flincher to leave. Then they went back to laughing.

". . . twenty-seven amendments," Stingleberry squeaked, sounding less like a teacher and more like a small, frightened ferret. This made the kids laugh even harder. Sitting in the back row, Penelope did not laugh, because she felt sorry for Stingleberry, and because she had no one to laugh with.

During recess, while Penelope read her book, the Funkhauser twins—who had the combined intellect of a small shrub—waltzed up and recited this charming little nursery rhyme:

> *"Penelope, smell-o-pee, big old snore-a*
> *Her head is off in Pooba Pora,*
> *She read a book*
> *And didn't look*
> *And walked into a big old door-a."*

The twins ran off, giggling and yanking each other's ears. But Penelope never looked up. Instead, she finished her book, closing it with the same mix of satisfaction and melancholy that comes with ending any good story. When she finally did look up, she was surprised to find herself on a school playground, alone on a seesaw, her feet on the ground, as there was nobody across from her to balance her weight.

If you were to walk into Glacier Cove Academy's sixth-grade classroom an hour later, you would see twenty-three kids goofing around. You would see one purple-faced teacher standing on his head and attempting to drink a glass of water upside down. And, if you looked closely, you would see a girl sitting at her desk in the back row, staring out the window, her eyes searching for *something*. Something big. Something different.

Dinner that night: turnip casserole, a glass of turnip juice, and a turnip.

All three Marches ate in silence until Miles cleared his throat. "Last chance for today's riddle. What word becomes shorter when you add two letters to it? Come on, people."

Penelope, whose brain was still somewhere in the fjords of Provincia with Nicola Torland, didn't hear him. She imagined herself on a mountain, bow and arrow in hand. *I want to be the plucky heroine. . . .* If only she could have her memory wiped so that she could read the book again for the first time.

When she looked up from her plate, she saw Miles and her father staring at her curiously.

"What did you say?" Miles asked.

Penelope didn't realize she'd said anything.

"You want to be lucky like Marilyn?"

"Miles, let it go."

"A ducky named Carolyn?"

"Please stop."

"Come on, you know me. I never stop."

Penelope blushed. "I said, I want to be the plucky heroine. The courageous girl who solves the mystery. Saves the day, beats the bad guy. Using nothing more than her wits and cunning."

Miles stifled a laugh.

"Is it really that funny?" Penelope asked.

"It's not funny at all." A giggle escaped between the fingers over his mouth.

"Thanks a lot."

"Come on, Pen. You're a space case. You have no cunning."

"I have cunning. I'm full of cunning!"

"Under the right circumstances, I could totally see you saving a library. A bookstore, maybe."

Penelope felt an angry warmth seep into her cheeks. She pushed the turnip around on her plate and pretended her feelings were not hurt.

"Short," she blurted out.

"What's short?"

"The riddle," Penelope answered. "What word becomes shorter when you add two letters to it? The answer is *short*. By the way, you've got turnip juice on your chin."

Miles wiped his chin and grinned. "Okay. You're a little plucky."

The next day, it all began.

CHAPTER 3

After school on Wednesdays, Miles had Escapology Club. Escapology Club had one other member, an asthmatic kid who showed up only to avoid his mother and read comic books in peace while Miles practiced straitjacket escapes and lock-picking relatively unbothered. That was how Penelope came to be walking home alone.

Engulfed in a new book, she let her feet do all the work. They knew the way: left on Gusty Hallow Road, right on Boulder Gulch, cut across the alley behind Oceanic, come out on Watermill Boulevard. After passing Edinburgh's Discount Footwear ("Buy one boot, get the other free!"), she absentmindedly peered through the window of Wanamaker's Fortune-Telling Emporium.

Between the blinds, she spied her classmate Coral Wanamaker, who had been absent from school the past two days. A tiny thing with raven-black hair and a black coat and eyes that would be piercing if she could look at anyone directly, Coral swept the floor like a dancing ghost. She was so frail, so pale—even by Glacier Cove's standards—that Penelope thought she could almost see through her.

Coral Wanamaker was a mystery. She gave the world only four facts to go on:

1. She always wore black.
2. She hadn't voluntarily spoken in class since first grade.
3. She had cut the fingertips off her black gloves, apparently so she could bite her nails and spit the slivers everywhere.
4. Her grandmother was Stella Wanamaker, the kooky lady who ran Wanamaker's Fortune-Telling Emporium.

That was enough for her classmates. Coral did not poke fun at Penelope for the simple reason that she was too busy getting teased herself. Kids constantly shoved ice cubes down the back of Coral's snow pants or thumped her brittle ears. They gave her wet willies and dry willies and every other kind of willy imaginable. Compared to the nasty insults she heard, the taunts directed at Penelope qualified as gentle ribbing.

One might think that two victims, as Penelope and Coral obviously were, would gravitate toward one another. Band together, take solace in their common misery, that sort of thing.

But Coral seemed to believe that joining forces was not a good strategy. In fact, it was the *worst* strategy, for it would only double the attention, and the last thing Coral wanted was more attention. She made herself absent even when she was right there. So she ignored Penelope, and they suffered alone.

Any child who has been bullied knows there are usually only three ways to endure the agony: One is to wait it out and pray it goes away. Another is to tell an adult. The third is to fight back. Penelope had chosen the first option, and she was patient enough to see it through. But no one could tell what course of action Coral Wanamaker had chosen.

For all Penelope knew, the strange girl was plotting her revenge.

"Your fortune, child?"

Penelope nearly jumped. Blocking the doorway of Wanamaker's Fortune-Telling Emporium was Stella Wanamaker. The old lady's jet-black eyebrows resembled two tarantulas, and she had sharpened her fingernails to points that could slice glass. Her white hair was pulled back so tight Penelope could see the scalp underneath, pink and splotchy.

But the weirdest thing was Stella's eyes. One dreamy, unfocused, and gray as ash, fixed on something far in the distance. The other, a crystal-clear blue, locked in, fierce and unblinking.

"Have you had your fortune told, child?" the old woman slurred, her meaty breath producing temporary clouds.

Penelope had not, and she certainly didn't want this to be her first time. "I don't have any money."

"Inside, come." Stella gestured into her shop, making clear this was not a request. "Now."

The parlor, a dusty space full of candles and billowy sheets, looked exactly as Penelope had always imagined it. A flickering light revealed ancient tapestries on the walls and a wobbly table; a sickly bird squawked in a cage in the corner. The air smelled of melted wax. Farther back, a stove and a purple bead curtain led to what Penelope assumed was Coral and her grandmother's apartment.

In the middle of it all, cheeks pink and warm, broom still in hand, was Coral. She looked to her grandmother—equal parts confusion and embarrassment—for some hint as to why her classmate was here. But Stella had already drifted behind the counter to grab two candles and a brass bowl.

"Half a brain," said Stella through a thick accent and a tongue so heavy it barely moved. "Visions, predictions, dangers—all there to see, for any fool with half a brain. Grab a child's palm! Stare into a crystal ball! But the future?" She clucked her tongue, making a noise that sounded like a rusty key scraping in the wrong lock. "There are more precise ways of seeing into the forever." She handed Penelope a red candle and a black candle. "Place them in the bowl."

With shaking hands, Penelope laid the candles carefully next to each other.

Stella rolled her blue eye and grunted in disgust.

"Stand them up," Coral said.

Penelope—startled by the fact that Coral had

broken her silence and that her voice sounded fairly ordinary—stood the candles on end.

Stella slid the bowl onto an oven burner. The candles began to shrink and melt together, until they were nothing more than a thick, dark liquid bubbling in the bowl. Stella poured the liquid into a container of ice water, and the wax hardened into intricate patterns.

"Bored," Stella said in a flat voice. "You are bored. Hungry. And lonely. Very, very lonely. Afraid to take chances."

Penelope said nothing. She could feel Coral looking at her.

"Here," Stella said, pointing to what looked like the outline of a small shoe. "A stranger has entered your life? A new acquaintance?"

"No."

"It will happen." The old woman's expression changed slightly before returning to normal, or as normal as her expression could be. "Do not trust this stranger."

"Why?"

"This section? You see? A lion. Means an unpleasant situation developing. Right here: umbrella image, symbolizes trouble to come. And here— Oh . . ."

"What is it?"

Stella's face darkened. Horror oozed from her body in foul waves. She backed away from the bowl. "We are finished."

Penelope's chest tightened. "What do you see?"

"Finished. Go."

Penelope looked into the bowl. "I don't see anything."

"I think you'd better leave," Coral interjected.

Penelope studied the old lady. So confident a moment earlier, she could not look at Penelope now. Not even with her good eye.

"No," Penelope said. "Not until she tells me what she saw."

"You go!" the old lady shrieked. *"Now!"*

Penelope couldn't move until her feet, the only part of her body not paralyzed with fear, goaded the rest of her toward the door. Her fingers came to life just enough to push it open so she could slide through.

Stella locked the door behind Penelope and watched through a crack in the blinds until the girl had disappeared down the street.

Coral turned to her grandmother. "What was *that*?"

"Never . . ." Stella lifted the blind once more to

make sure the girl was really gone. "Never in all my years have I seen this."

The wax in the bowl had changed considerably. It now resembled an endless puff of clouds surrounding the unmistakable face of a ghostly, hungry figure, gnarled and menacing.

"What does it mean?" Coral asked.

"Some . . . *thing* . . . is threatening the girl. A dark image from the past—a creature very powerful— seeks her. This being will not stop until the girl has been found. And dealt with."

Coral stared into her grandmother's good eye, which was closed for once and shielded by a baggy, pocked layer of skin. When the eye finally opened, it locked on Coral. Not a word passed between Stella and Coral, but each knew what the other was thinking. It didn't surprise the girl when Stella cleared her throat and uttered the three words she knew were coming, but they still chilled her as deeply as any three words possibly could.

"It is time."

CHAPTER 4

Thoughts exploded in Penelope's head as she tottered home.

That crazy old lady!

She has no right to scare kids like that!

Who in their right mind believes in this nonsense?

What did she see?

When she turned onto Cloudburst Avenue, Penelope didn't give much thought to the faint whisper that faded into the wind. It was less a whisper than the *idea* of a whisper, and she hardly noticed it over her boots squeaking in the snow.

Then she heard it again. Yes, definitely a whisper.

A dark shiver plummeted from her neck to her

tailbone. Penelope glanced in all directions. She was alone. "Who's there?"

She had picked up her pace, moving as fast as she could without actually running, when she heard a voice that seemed to originate from nowhere and everywhere.

"*COME.*"

Now she began to jog, then run, then sprint as fast as she could, her feet tingling. But the ice in Glacier Cove did not forgive reckless movements, and Penelope's feet slipped out from under her. Next thing she knew—*wham!*—she was facedown on the sidewalk.

She staggered to her feet, and that was when she saw the furry white dog blocking her path.

Penelope tried to go one way and it blocked her.

She tried the other way. Again the dog would not let her pass.

The two of them studied each other for what seemed like a long time. The dog's gigantic head and animated eyes mesmerized Penelope in a way she could not explain. When he started toward the street—with a sense of purpose, unlike normal pooches with their dumb sniffing or thoughtless loping—Penelope thought he seemed almost . . . dignified. The dog stopped in the middle of Cloudburst Avenue and dug his claws into the ice.

Approaching from the east was a small gray car, careening and sliding on the ice. From the west, an even smaller and grayer car, also lurching out of control. They sped toward each other—and toward the dog—as if pulled by a magnetic force. Nothing could stop them.

"Look out!" Penelope hollered, and started to run toward the dog. But the slippery ice made her sprint a sort of half run, half tumble.

As the cars hurtled toward each other, the dog caught Penelope's eye, and . . . *Did he wink?* Penelope dove onto the road headfirst, her belly scraping the ground as she shoved the yelping dog out of danger. And put herself directly into danger.

Both drivers, surprised to find a girl lying face-down in the street, blared their horns. They swerved. They braked.

HOOOOOOONNNK—

SCREEEEEEEEEEEEECH—

Penelope covered her head, bracing for impact.

But it never came. When she looked up, one car had plowed into the snowbank on her left. The other had embedded itself in the bank on her right.

They had missed her. And somehow, they had missed each other.

Both drivers jumped from their cars, fists clenched, smiling phony smiles. "So sorry, neighbor! My car slid right into your lane."

"No, no. I'm such a numb-noggin! I slid into yours."

"Nonsense! I'm the numb-noggin. Please, let me pay for the damages."

"Don't be ridiculous! If anyone's the numb-noggin, it's me."

Once the drivers finally agreed they had both been numb-noggins, they made sure Penelope was okay and proceeded to dig their cars from the snow. Eventually, they shook hands, exchanged turnips, and drove off swearing under their breath.

Penelope was left sitting on the curb, wondering what had just happened. And how she had survived.

The dog, amused by the course of events, licked Penelope's face. Then he shook the snow from his fur, trotted back out into the street, and planted himself in the same spot as before.

Penelope laughed. "Get out of the road, you dumb mutt!"

The dog yawned and licked himself.

Penelope opened her bag. "Do you like turnips?"

The dog bared his teeth. No turnips.

She hooked a finger under the dog's collar and dragged him to the edge of the snowy lawn, looking for an identification tag. Nothing.

"Where do you live?"

The dog nodded and trotted off.

Penelope followed him down one block and then another, through an alley and across a lawn to another lawn, struggling to keep up and wondering if she was supposed to. She was relieved when the dog finally stopped. "You live here?" she asked.

The dog barked and wagged his fluffy tail, and Penelope realized she was standing, once again, in front of the Ice House. The familiar dread seeped into her bones.

From this close, the house looked even more ominous, and Penelope didn't want to get closer. But what if the dog—who must be the mighty Wolfknuckle— wandered back into the street? Then what? Another senseless rescue?

Fine. She took a deep breath and walked to the porch steps.

"That's as far as I'll go," she whispered. But Wolf- knuckle whimpered until she nudged him onto the porch, the ice floorboards creaking with every step. When she stopped, Penelope could hear only two things: the *TICK-TICK-TICK* of the white clock over the door and the *KA-THUMP, KA-THUMP* of her heart through layers of clothes.

A line of sweat ran down her face as she inched toward the door and reached for the knocker, a dirty old thing hanging with icicles. Just as she was about to lift it, Wolfknuckle emitted a sound that startled Penelope. To the average person, the noise may have sounded like a bark. But what Penelope heard was:

"*LOOK.*"

Wolfknuckle pointed his wet nose at a square opening near the bottom of the door, one of those little plastic doggy entrances that swing in and out so a pet can come and go as he pleases.

"So go in," Penelope whispered.

Wolfknuckle didn't move.

Penelope looked over her shoulder to make sure no one was watching, then stuffed the big dog through the little door. Despite his girth and his protests, she managed to get him inside, the poor dog's claws *click-clack*ing on some unknown surface on the other side.

But as Penelope went to pull her arm out, something stopped her. The harder she pulled, the tighter it clung to her exposed wrist.

Maybe it was the terror of the moment, but Penelope felt certain that on the other side of the door, wrapped around her wrist with the strength of a thousand teeth-gnashing lions, was someone's—or something's—hand, cold and rough. She could not break free.

All at once, the hand jerked her through the doggy door, backpack and all, leaving nothing but Penelope's screams echoing up and down the silent block.

CHAPTER 5

The first thing Penelope saw inside the house was not a hand but a foot, kicking the door shut behind her.

The foot belonged to a stooped old man, no taller than Penelope, wearing a lab coat and goggles and clutching ... good Lord, was that a chain saw? His hair looked like an ancient dollar bill, greenish gray and crinkled, and when he opened his mouth, what Penelope saw scared her more than the chain saw did.

He did not have sharp teeth, nor did he have black teeth.

He had no teeth at all.

"You'le tlespassing on plivate ploperty!" this gnome of a man hissed, his cracked lips smacking against his gums.

"I . . . I . . . ," Penelope ventured, but nothing more dared escape her mouth.

"Dool you know lat happens to little hirls who tlespass on my ploperty?" The man waved the chain saw to and fro and reached into his pocket.

"Please . . . please don't hurt me," Penelope stammered. "My name is Penelope March and I live on Broken Branch Lane. I . . . Your dog was in danger. . . ."

She looked to Wolfknuckle, hoping he could somehow explain the situation to this madman. But the dog was watching the scene curiously, as though nothing like this had ever happened and he was interested to see how it would play out.

The man's face softened. He reached into the pocket of his lab coat and pulled out something pink and gruesome—false teeth?—and slid them into his mouth with a loud suck. "Ah, much better," he said. "My utmost apologies. I'm always a bit testy without the old choppers. Now, tell me, what are you chattering about? What in blazes was your arm doing in my foyer?"

"Wolfknuckle," Penelope said. "He ran into the street and nearly got hit by a car."

"Wolfknuckle? Who is this Wolfknuckle? Your imaginary friend? I most certainly hope so, because as far as imaginary friend names go, that may be the best I've ever heard."

"No! Your dog. Him."

The old man looked at his dog. "Wolfknuckle? Wolfknuckle!" He erupted into hearty peals of laughter. "I've never heard such a misnomer. That yellow-bellied mutt faints at the mere mention of blood. His name is Henry. But I'll have to start calling him by his new name."

As Wolfknuckle/Henry hung his enormous head and slunk away in shame, the old man took off his goggles. "I," he said with an exaggerated bow, "am Ore9n Buzzardstock. *O-R-E-9-N*. The nine is silent. What did you say your name was?"

"Penelope. March."

"Pleased to meet you, Penelope March." He extended the chain saw as if it were his hand.

Penelope did not shake the chain saw. She had finally noticed the peculiar surroundings into which she had been pulled. Just beyond the foyer was a giant ice gallery—a colorful wonderland teeming with elevated nooks and lofts and upside-down forts. Long twisting slides morphed into tunnels, which gave way to ladders and sideways staircases curlicuing at impossible angles. Some led to balconies. Others led directly to the ceiling. Others led to nowhere at all.

Among them, sculpted with obvious care, were dozens of bizarre moments frozen in ice and time. A grizzly bear in a barber's chair, getting his fur trimmed and reading a newspaper. A romantic scene between an elf and a slice of Swiss cheese. A tuxedoed gentleman with three chins playing three violins. Each sculpture was so detailed and realistic that Penelope felt oddly shy, as though she were in a crowded room rather than alone with a stranger. This was the work of a madman. Or a genius. Both, maybe.

"How did you do all this?"

"The lost art of ice sculpture," Buzzardstock said. "My father, Alex5ei Buzzardstock, taught me. Magnificent artist, Alex5ei. His father, Dmit3ri Leonov Buzzardstock, taught him. Ice is all we Buzzardstocks know, really. Here." He handed Penelope a chisel. "Take off your gloves and give it a try."

The tool was razor-sharp and heavy in her hands, and she wondered what kind of man would hand a weapon to a child he had just met. Or any other child.

"Don't be timid," he said, gesturing at a block of ice sitting on a worktable. "Give it a go."

Penelope took a tentative poke at the ice, spraying slivers of frost here and there. She tried again, and a chunk chipped off in a perfect straight line.

"Well now," Buzzardstock said. "It appears you're a natural."

Penelope blushed. "How do you make the colors?"

"Oh, a variety of ways. I add special dyes. Gels. The blood of children."

Penelope gripped the chisel tighter.

Buzzardstock giggled. "I've heard the stories. I'm a vampire. I'm a reincarnated demon child. I'm an opium-addled zombie cannibal. I'm half man, half cobra, half biscuit, which makes me a hundred percent creature, fifty percent pastry, and a mathematical impossibility, to boot. That's my favorite!"

Penelope giggled and looked around the room. "This is . . ."

"Do you like it? Oh, even if you don't, please say you do. I've grown quite needy in my old age."

"I think it's the most amazing thing I've ever seen."

Buzzardstock beamed. "Ah, a child with taste. Not like the pea-headed hooligans who throw turnips at my windows. Oh, how I despise turnips, their bulbous taproot and the revolting insult masquerading as flavor contained in their foul, acrid flesh. Don't much like the kids either."

Penelope ran her fingers along a sculpted pool table. The balls were little ice pomegranates and hand grenades, and reaching from each corner pocket was a decrepit hand. "How long have you been doing this?"

"The better part of thirty-one years." Buzzardstock sighed. "Who knows how long it will last? Time is tighter than my portly dog's collar. But that's the beauty of ice sculpture: fleeting magnificence remains the most poignant magnificence."

Penelope didn't understand what he meant.

"I feel that I owe you a favor," Buzzardstock said. "What with your saving my dog—what was it, Bloodbutter?—from certain disaster. Come to my kitchen for conversation and ale. No, wait. Perhaps you're too young for ale. Conversation, then."

"I should be getting home," she said. "I have a lot of homework."

"*Homework?*" Buzzardstock scoffed. "What does one learn from homework besides spelling words and multiplication tables and other pointless nonsense?"

This comment stung Penelope, though she wasn't sure why, considering she also thought homework was a waste of time.

39

Buzzardstock bit his chapped lip and arranged what was left of his hair. "I'm sorry," he said. "I don't get many visitors here. School and homework are terribly important, if for no reason than they teach you about the strange ways of adults who resent your youth and wish nothing more than to end it as quickly as possible. Why don't you come back when you have more time? I'll give you the grand tour."

"I'd like that."

"Wonderful! If you'll excuse me for a moment, I'll return shortly and show you out." Buzzardstock scurried down a corridor that seemed to go on forever, his little work boots squeaking out a choppy drumbeat on the floor.

I'm alone, Penelope thought. *In the Ice House. What a weird afternoon.*

She saw a flyer on the ice coffee table. Penelope smoothed it out and read the large Gothic print:

TIME IS RUNNING OUT.
GLACIER COVE IS DOOMED!

A tingle scurried up her neck. The message was frightening enough on its own, but something about the lettering, which looked ancient and authoritative, chilled her bones. Before she could read the small print, Penelope saw something else on the table, cradled in a nest of crinkled aluminum foil.

A cookie.

It might've been chocolate chip or oatmeal. With its dull color and surface of lumps and craters, it looked more like the moon than any cookie she had ever seen. As she glanced around the room at the sculptures and thought of the man who had created them—the same man who had most likely baked this cookie—her responsible side took charge. She couldn't possibly . . .

Stella Wanamaker's thick accent tumbled into Penelope's head: *A stranger has entered your life. . . . Do not trust this stranger.*

On cue, Penelope's stomach spoke up with a yawning growl. She was so hungry. The thought of another meal of turnip stew angered her belly. What could one bite hurt? Buzzardstock would never notice.

She reached for the aluminum, her fingers inches away—

"Thank you once again for saving my hapless canine," brayed Buzzardstock, who had reappeared. "I'm sorry to have kept you waiting, but now I must resume my work. Pleased to meet you, Penelope March, and I eagerly await your return." He extended his wrinkled hand to Penelope, who had pulled hers far from the cookie.

With that, Ore9n Buzzardstock slid the goggles over his eyes, cranked up the chain saw, and returned to work on his latest sculpture, which appeared to be a team of penguins in military uniforms bowling against a team of rhinoceri—and winning, based on the smug looks on the penguins' faces.

Penelope grabbed the cookie and ran home.

It wasn't until she made it back to her room on Broken Branch Lane, dripping with cold sweat, that she noticed she had forgotten her gloves.

CHAPTER 6

"If you don't eat it, I will."

"Oh no, you won't."

"One bite."

"No bites."

"A crumb?"

"No crumbs, Miles."

"Come on, Pen!"

"No."

Miles and Penelope stood in line behind dozens of kids lugging makeshift sleds. Most had garbage can lids or ratty old plastic seats. One girl hoisted a laundry basket over her head. All had climbed the same slippery ice ladder to the top of Ivory Shelf, Glacier Cove's peak. To get back down, they had three paths: Body Bag Glades (long, winding), Nose Dive (short, steep), or Satan's Elevator (fast, pants-wetting terrifying). Penelope had never collected enough nerve to try Satan's Elevator, and judging by the screams of kids who had, she never would.

Miles reached for Penelope's pocket. She slapped his hand away. "Don't. Touch. The cookie." Penelope tightened her grip on the foil package.

"Why'd you take it if you're not going to eat it?"

"I wasn't thinking."

"Come on. It's just a cookie."

"It's *my* cookie. I'll decide what to do with it."

"I think I might have to make a scene, then."

"Miles, don't—"

"ATTENTION, IVORY SHELF! MY SISTER, PENELOPE MARCH, HAS GONE CUCKOO!"

A few kids laughed, but most ignored the outburst. Miles March was always yelling random things or humming along with a tune no one else heard, never worrying—or even noticing—whether anyone heard him.

"Thanks a lot." Penelope peeked over the sea of hats and scarves snaking around the Ivory Shelf.

"What are we doing here? I hate the Shelf. My hands are freezing."

"Hey, Cohen! Keep the line moving!" Miles hollered.

Cohen shuffled forward. "Yeah, keep your lips moving, March."

Miles turned to Penelope. "Tell me again."

"Which part?"

"Every part."

For the third time, Penelope recounted all she could remember about the strange afternoon. The dog, the sculptures, the flyer, Buzzardstock's false teeth, everything. She described her eerie encounter with Stella Wanamaker and how the old woman had said a stranger would enter her life and he couldn't be trusted. Each time she repeated the details, it felt more like a dream. The only proof was in her coat pocket, folded up in aluminum foil.

"I want to see the Ice House," Miles said. "When you go back to get your gloves, I'm coming too."

"That's not a good idea."

"Why not?"

Penelope shook her head. "I think we should tell Dad."

Miles groaned. Their father was not the kind of man who would encourage his children to eat a cookie baked by a stranger with green hair and a chain saw, much less spend time in such a man's home.

"Don't tell Dad." Miles crept closer to the front of the line. "If we tell Dad, he'll say no, and that'll be that."

Penelope knew her brother was right. She had an anxious feeling about Buzzardstock that she couldn't explain. Though he seemed harmless enough, and she certainly did not want to kiss the Ice House and its mysteries goodbye, something was not right about him.

"Fine, I won't tell." Penelope set down her sled at the top of Body Bag Glades. That was when she turned and saw Coral Wanamaker behind them in line, alone, holding a worn square of cardboard and staring right at Penelope. Penelope waved, more in shock at seeing Coral than anything else.

Coral waved back, but instead of moving her hand, she moved the rest of her body and kept her hand still. It was as though she had never waved at anyone in her life and wasn't sure how.

"Here we go," said Miles, oblivious. He trundled over to Satan's Elevator and pretzeled his lanky body onto his sled. "So, what about the Ice House?"

Penelope snapped back to attention. "I'll think about it."

They launched their bodies down their separate paths, adding to the chorus of noise on the mountain.

Think about the Ice House Penelope did. She spent hours tossing and turning in her hammock that night, listening to the snow swirl outside.

Miles had been sleeping in his handcuffs lately and waking up periodically to thrash and scrape himself free. Tonight he lay fast asleep, arms pinned behind his back.

As quietly as she could, Penelope reached into her coat pocket, feeling the creased aluminum. Before she could pull the package out, a noise echoed from the kitchen.

Penelope crept into the kitchen to find her father slumped in his chair, his beefy fingers clutching an empty glass. His head lay on the table, a puddle of foamy purple drool spooling from his mouth.

Penelope sighed. What little money their family had, her father earned as a turnip icer, the most thankless job on Glacier Cove. Basically, it involved chipping away at the ice until he could pull up the turnips miraculously growing underneath.

Backbreaking work, even on a good day. Most of his paycheck went toward buying food for his children and himself, which meant more turnips.

But Russell March also bought bottles of Purple Lightning. A foul alcohol made from a mixture of fermented turnips and other repulsive rubbish, Purple Lightning turned him into someone else entirely. And that someone was not a person Penelope wanted to know. While he would never hurt Penelope or Miles, he had once punched a kitchen cabinet in a rage. The hole left by his fist was still there; in fact, it was one of Miles's favorite places to leave notes for Penelope: a constant reminder of their father's unpredictability.

Tonight, after making sure he was breathing, Penelope wiped the drool from her father's face, put a pillow under his head, and gently removed his boots. She allowed herself a moment to resent him before kissing his sweaty head. "I love you, Dad," she whispered.

"I love you, Angela," he garbled.

Penelope hadn't heard him speak her mother's name out loud in years. To hear it now pricked her heart. Suddenly, the thought of returning to her hammock saddened her, as did the certainty that her father would not remember this in the morning. He would be distant and drive off in his dented car to work in the turnip fields. So she sat down on the living room couch and pulled the foil package from her pocket.

In the dark, it looked like any other cookie, lumpy and heavy. Maybe one bite—

No, a voice in her head said. *This is a bad idea. Don't do it.*

Yes, another voice said. *This is a great idea. Do it!*

No.

Yes.

No!

Would you shut up?

No, you shut up!

Eventually the two voices began interrupting each other and screaming in Penelope's head so loudly she was certain that Miles would hear them from the next room. There was only one way to shut them out. She picked up the first book she could find and read until her eyes stung.

CHAPTER 7

Breakfast the next day was like any other, with all three Marches working on their bowls of Turnip Flakes in their usual spots. If Russell March had any recollection of the night before, he didn't show it. The only hints of the evening's activities were his bloodshot eyes and an empty bottle peeking from the garbage can.

"You plow this morning?" their father grunted.

"Whole south side," Miles said between mouthfuls. "What a waste of time. It's snowing again."

"No honest work is a waste of time."

Miles snorted. "Only someone who hasn't driven a snowplow in twenty-five years would say that." Glacier Cove's kids took Plower's Ed in fifth grade.

If they passed their test, they were expected to pilot the town's snowplows for at least a year, starting at the age of eleven, often rising at three a.m. to clear the streets before the rest of the town woke up. Adults considered plowing an honor and a rite of passage. Of course, the kids hated it. No child in his or her right mind continued to plow once they turned twelve. Penelope had struggled through Plower's Ed, done her year, and promptly thrown away her license.

"It should've only taken an hour, but the blade is duller than a butter knife," Miles said. "And I think the clutch is leaking hydraulic fluid again."

"You tell Mr. Pisciotta?" Russell asked.

"Yeah. I don't think he can hear me through all that earwax."

"Dad," Penelope said. "Do you know Ore9n Buzzardstock?"

Miles dropped his spoon in his bowl, unleashing a tsunami of milk.

"The old man with the green hair? In that ridiculous house?" Russell asked. "He went to school with Grandpa Bennett. Odd fella."

"Odd how?"

"Oh, I don't know. One time—this was long before you were born—he took off his clothes in the

51

middle of a blizzard and climbed the Bank Tower Building, naked, and sang 'Happy Birthday' to himself. Wasn't even his birthday. Didn't look especially happy, either."

Penelope giggled. She had no doubt that Buzzardstock had done exactly that. "Do you think he's dangerous?"

"Dangerous? Don't imagine so. People like him, they're in their own world. Not so interested in the rest of us. What's this all about?"

"I don't know. I walk past that house every day and wonder."

Miles tried to catch Penelope's eye, but she refused to meet his stare. Their father didn't notice the exchange. As far as he was concerned, the conversation was over.

"Dad," Penelope said.

Russell gave his daughter a dead look. *What now?*

"Do you ever get tired of turnips? Just . . . I don't know . . . wish there was something else out there?"

Russell said nothing for a good thirty seconds. "Wishing ain't gonna make it so. Now eat your breakfast."

• • •

Penelope sat on the seesaw with a new book, but she was having trouble getting into it for three reasons:

1. It was not Nicola Torland.
2. She couldn't stop thinking about Buzzardstock.
3. Her butt might have frozen to the seat.

Recess had nearly ended when Penelope felt her side of the seesaw rise ever so slightly off the ground. Startled, she looked up from her book.

Across from her, barely large enough to lift the seesaw, sat Coral. "Do you and your brother get along?" she blurted out.

"Yes," said Penelope, confused. "We do."

"Yeah, I thought so. It seems like you like each other."

Penelope closed her book. "He's probably my best friend. My only friend."

Coral began working on her thumbnail, flattening it between her chattering teeth. "I wish I had a brother. Or a sister. Or anything, really. Sometimes I go days without talking to anyone."

"What about your grandmother?"

"She doesn't count. I make her dinner and wash her clothes, but she's not interested in me. Mostly I do what she tells me and keep my mouth shut."

"Is she . . ." Penelope wanted to say *crazy*. "Is she nice?"

"Nice?" Coral spat out her thumbnail. "I don't know. I mean, she'd give you the shirt off her back, but then she'd keep reminding you how cold she was. And if you tried to give her the shirt back, she wouldn't take it."

Penelope laughed. "What about your parents? Where—"

"Never knew 'em."

"What happened?"

"Don't know. I've pieced a few things together. There was some incident when I was little, and it had something to do with me." Coral looked at Penelope. "What about your parents?"

"My dad loves me, but he's always sad. I wish I had known him . . . before."

"Before what?"

"My mom died when I was a baby. I never knew her. It's like my father thinks she belongs to him and he won't share any memories with anyone."

Coral nodded. "Why are adults so selfish?"

The bell rang, signaling the end of recess, but neither girl wanted to end the conversation. They climbed off the seesaw only when some seventh graders began throwing snowballs at them. Though neither Penelope nor Coral said a word, both girls defended themselves—and each other—by throwing snowballs back.

"I was wondering when you'd return, my dear girl."

Buzzardstock gestured into his home with a dramatic wave. He was dressed just as he had been before, in lab coat and goggles, though the emerald-green hair poking from his mole seemed to be growing faster than the rest of his hair. "You left your gloves in my possession," he said. "As we all know, it does not pay to be gloveless in Glacier Cove."

Penelope smiled. "May we come in?"

Buzzardstock glanced at Miles. He hadn't noticed him on the porch beside Penelope. "And who is this strapping young lout? Your bodyguard? Your chauffeur? A brutish suitor who doesn't deserve you?"

"I'm Miles," he said nervously, and snuck a peek at Buzzardstock. The boy had a way of looking sideways at anyone over the age of thirty as if secretly studying them for hints, for tics, for anything that would explain how they'd gotten so boring and unimaginative. But Buzzardstock's clear eyes were the opposite of dead. They danced in their sockets, emitting a glinty blue spark so bright and curious that Miles felt compelled to look away. "Penelope's brother."

"Miles." Buzzardstock rubbed his chin. "And how, pray tell, do I know you're not among the scruffy buttered ruffians who hurl root vegetables at my door with such boneheaded glee?"

"I only throw turnips at rats and school windows."

"Oh, I like this one," Buzzardstock said, pumping Miles's hand enthusiastically. "Please enter my not-so-humble abode." He led them toward the living room, past a new sculpture of a conveyor belt churning out ice doughnuts sprinkled with what appeared to be very small and angry gnomes. "Have a seat and I'll procure the gloves." Buzzardstock disappeared into another room.

Penelope and Miles stopped in the doorway of the living room. Sitting in Buzzardstock's Freezy-Boy recliner, Wolfknuckle on her lap, was Coral Wanamaker.

Penelope almost dropped her backpack. "Are you *friends* with Buzzardstock?"

Coral nibbled her thumbnail. "Never met him before."

"So what are you doing here?"

Coral spat the thumbnail at her feet and lowered her voice. "My grandmother asked me to come. Said Buzzardstock was lonely and would love the company."

Before Penelope had a chance to consider whether this was true, Buzzardstock reappeared with the gloves. "Here you go. Please, please, sit down."

"Mr. Buzzardstock—" Penelope began.

"No, no, no, no, no, no. No! Call me Ore9n. The nine is silent."

"Ore9n," Penelope said, trying out the name like a tart slice of peach. She looked at Coral, then back at Buzzardstock. "Could we speak privately?"

Buzzardstock shook his head. "There will be no secrets within these walls. Secrecy is the devil's broth. With a side of boiled turnips. Until a moment ago, I didn't know this delightful girl—Coral, is it?—but now she is my guest, just as you are, and I am compelled to welcome her as such."

Penelope watched Coral, whose face remained maddeningly neutral. But Wolfknuckle's sigh of contentment on her lap was somehow reassuring. Penelope turned to Buzzardstock. "Last time I was here, I saw a strange piece of paper. A pamphlet."

Buzzardstock fiddled with a chisel. "Is that so?"

"It said something about how Glacier Cove was doomed."

The old man's face turned white.

"It also said time was running out," she added.

"Oh dear," Buzzardstock said in voice so weak it was almost a whisper. "Oh no. No, you most certainly should not have seen that."

CHAPTER 8

Ore9n Buzzardstock sat on the floor, his spindly legs spread in a perfect V, and inhaled deeply. "What I'm about to tell you may sound absurd," he said. "Just hear me out, all right?"

And with that, the old man began.

"For thousands of years, deep-sea colonies lined the floor of the Southern Ocean. Beautiful, lush kingdoms filled with thousands of species of fish and water nymphs and other creatures—all coexisting.

"A young mermaid named Makara Nyx lived with her parents in Syreniopolis, the largest colony. Seemed like a normal mermaid: gorgeous, high-strung, a bit aloof. On her sixteenth birthday, Makara Nyx's parents died. Some say it was a suicide pact, and she found the bodies in a bed of kelp. Others believe she killed them. Either way, their deaths affected the girl in a profound way."

Coral opened her mouth to speak, then thought better of it and sank into the Freezy-Boy recliner.

"A few days later, a cod passing by Syreniopolis was shocked at what it found. The entire colony had been wiped out. Mermaids, mermen, children, grandparents, schools of fish, and generations of water nymphs—every living soul slaughtered. Syreniopolis had become a floating graveyard. And Nyx was gone."

Penelope felt a sharp twinge of anger. What kind of monster could kill her parents? She was stuck with a bitter father who kept her at a distance and a mother she never knew. She would've done anything for one normal parent, let alone two.

"In the coming years, similar tragedies befell the neighboring colonies," Buzzardstock continued. "Algarum Kingdom, Delphini, Pisce Dominion. All wiped out. Many thought some kind of plague had been responsible. But word spread around the ocean about Makara Nyx—the one survivor of Syreniopolis—and how she had begun to grow into something hideous and frightening: a shape-shifter.

"It was said Nyx could change herself into anything she desired: a seagull, a man, a cloud, a salad, anything. No one knew her true appearance. Some believed she resembled a giant manta ray with the tongue of a snake and the teeth of a shark. All of which made her impossible to find, let alone kill. She hid herself inside a massive crystal fortress along the ocean floor and ruled the waters."

At this point, Miles expressed his skepticism in the form of a snort.

Buzzardstock ignored him. "Of course, power attracts followers. Soon the waters were overrun with Nyx's disciples. Armies fought for territory until the waters ran red. The gods and goddesses decided that the only way to end the bloodshed was to split the ocean equally amongst themselves.

"Makara Nyx wanted more. She ate the fish in her province, as was her right, but then she started eating the fish in the next province. When the ruler of that province threatened her, she ate him too. On it went."

"Couldn't they stop her if they all joined together?" Penelope asked.

Buzzardstock smiled. "Eventually, a band of brave sea creatures attacked Nyx's crystal fortress.

A battle raged for three days and took many lives. Finally, they destroyed her fortress, but she somehow escaped. She vowed to slaughter every creature in the sea until there was no one left to challenge her. Which she attempted to do. She devoured so much of the ocean that whole species disappeared forever.

"Now, fish are salty, and gods even saltier. As a result, Nyx was always thirsty. So she started drinking the water. Then she decided the water wasn't cold enough, so she gathered all the ice she could find, broke it into millions of pieces, and spread it around the ocean. Icebergs.

"As Makara Nyx aged, the cold water began to hurt her teeth. It didn't help that she had never once brushed them . . . I'm not sure what she would have used—a tree branch? A diving board? Eventually, every gulp of water was so painful that she spat it back into the ocean before it could hit her foul tongue.

"That's when she began to melt each iceberg. One by one, they disappeared. That's where we are now. Her disciples are still out there, dozens of generations later, underwater and on land. They believe that someday the whole ocean will boil and everyone will die except the ones who pledge their devotion to Makara Nyx. And then they'll be reunited with their ancestors. So they do Nyx's foul bidding for no reason other than that it's what their parents taught them. And now, my children, I fear Makara Nyx has set her sights on Glacier Cove. Our home is nothing but an ice cube to her."

Penelope's head spun so fast she didn't know where to start. Instead she let Buzzardstock's words echo in her brain until they faded into memory. He'd told his story with weary resignation, as if he wished it weren't so, which of course made Penelope believe him even more. And Miles even less.

Where Coral stood on the matter, no one knew. Her expression of detached boredom never changed. Though by the time Buzzardstock finished, her tiny fingers, which had once been stroking Wolfknuckle, were squeezing and grinding the fleshy scruff of the poor dog's neck. When he yelped his displeasure, Coral jumped, as though she had completely forgotten the animal on her lap.

"What makes you think Glacier Cove is next?" Penelope asked.

"Call it a feeling," Buzzardstock said. "Granted, I'm a man of science, and this is pretty far from science. But I also know that the world is not always as it seems."

"Why now? If Makara Nyx has been around for ages, how has Glacier Cove survived as long as it has?"

"There's something I haven't told you. When the sea creatures exploded Nyx's fortress, shards of crystal floated to the surface. Other shards ended up on land. Some believe those shards, each roughly the size of a child's forearm, retain a certain magic and that any iceberg that possesses this magical crystal cannot be melted. These shards serve as Nyx's lifeblood. They give her strength. Without them, she ages. She has found and used every one of those shards until there was no energy left to draw from them. Except for one."

The old man paused and gently stroked a tuft of green hair poking from his mole. "And I have it. Hidden away where no one can find it."

CHAPTER 9

Behind Glacier Cove Academy, spread out in a smooth blue-white expanse, loomed Lake Trenchfoot. It had been frozen solid as long as anyone could remember.

Every Thursday afternoon, whether rain or snow or sleet or those little ice balls that stung your eyes upon contact, the entire middle school poured onto Lake Trenchfoot. There, one hundred twenty children of varying sizes and abilities engaged in one crowded and poorly organized sixty-on-sixty game of Cove Hockey. It was more controlled chaos than sport. Half the time you couldn't even find the puck.

For every kid who attempted to take the game seriously, ten more goofed around. There were sword fights and slap fights and tickle fights, kids chatting and flirting and throwing turnips. Penelope saw one boy flossing his teeth. She also saw Coral, as far from the action as she could possibly be, distressed that hockey rinks did not have corners in which to hide.

Though she didn't much care for hockey, Penelope wasn't bad at it. Even on absurdly congested ice, her skating was smooth, her stickhandling solid. On one occasion, she had shown surprising skill as a goalie, blocking every shot that came her way while reading a book in between the action. But kids inevitably fought over who got to play goalie, and she was never placed in the net again.

Today, Penelope pretended to play defense and skated in little circles, making not just figure eights, but also figure nines, and fours, and sixes.

A big knuckle-dragging doof named Ernest Kernwinkel was firing a wrist shot toward the goal when Teddy Bronconato, a cheerful rogue of a kid, skated up from behind and pantsed him. Ernest tumbled to the ground, skates twisted in his corduroys, revealing yellow long johns emblazoned with cartoon ducks. The kids hooted themselves hoarse as he struggled to pull up his pants and regain what little dignity he had left.

"I SAW THAT, BRONCONATO!" barked Mr. Burgle, the gym teacher. A muscled slab who seemed to scream even when he was whispering, Burgle pointed at Teddy. "HAVE A SEAT IN THE PENALTY BOX. TWO MINUTES."

Teddy skated off Lake Trenchfoot, smiling. It was worth the penalty to humiliate Kernwinkel. But before Teddy got to the penalty box—literally a cardboard box—he stopped short. "Hey," he said. "What the heck is March doing over there?"

Alone at the far end of the ice, Miles was waving his arms wildly.

At first glance, Penelope assumed her brother had encased himself in a straitjacket and was dislocating his shoulder again. One look at his terrified eyes told a different story. She saw his legs slipping out from under him.

Burgle skated toward Miles as fast as he could. "DON'T MOVE, MARCH!"

At that moment, a strange noise drifted through the air. A sizzle, like bacon crisping in a pan, crackled from one end of the ice to the other. Then a deafening *POP!*—a sonic boom so loud that half the kids jumped and the other half dove for cover. Screams echoed up and down Lake Trenchfoot.

In the chaos, everyone forgot about Miles March—that is, everyone but Penelope and Burgle, both of whom were grinding across the tundra toward him.

Then the ice cracked open beneath Miles and he was gone.

CHAPTER 10

The silence. That was all Penelope remembered later.

She didn't hear the kids' cries, or their skates clacking in the rush to get off the lake, or even Burgle's barbaric yelp. As Penelope skated toward the scene of the accident, time slowed down so much that she could hear the blood pulsing through her veins. At the spot where her brother had been standing a moment earlier, nothing was left but a small hole swirling with dark water and more cracks forming near her feet.

Penelope didn't notice Burgle stripping off his coat, nor did she hear his instructions: "GET THE KIDS OFF THE ICE AND PROMISE YOU

WON'T FOLLOW ME IN!" With that, the gym teacher took a deep breath and plunged into the hole.

The splash must have awakened Penelope. With a *whoosh,* as if emerging from a long tunnel, every sound came rushing back. And she knew one thing for certain: her brother was in big trouble, and so was Mr. Burgle.

"Listen to me!" a voice boomed, unfamiliar and confident. "Take off your scarves!" The voice, Penelope realized, was her own. Her hands were already undoing her own thick scarf while she skated to the edge of the lake.

No one moved.

"Stop standing around and do it!" Penelope barked.

Kids began unraveling their scarves and tossing them into an ever-growing mound of wool, polka dots, and snowflakes. Penelope quickly knotted each scarf together until she had two long ropes.

"What's she doing?" asked one kid.

"I don't know," said another. "But she'd better hurry."

Penelope handed Teddy Bronconato the makeshift rope. "Tie it around my leg. Tight. And fast."

While Teddy did as he was told, Penelope tied the other rope around her wrist and plopped down on her belly. She felt the leg rope to make sure it was tight enough. "Whatever you do," she told Teddy, "don't let go."

The kids watched her slide forward until she was about ten feet from the hole, at which point she threw the other end of the wrist rope down the hole.

Ice cracked in various places around her, causing some kids to scream. "Get her off the ice!" someone said. But no one moved. Penelope stayed glued on her belly and waited.

Nothing happened.

"Hold on tight!" she called. Before Teddy could object, Penelope shimmied toward the hole. The frost seeped through her coat as she thrust her bare hand into the hole as far as she could.

"Miles!" she screamed. "Take my hand!"

Penelope's fingers numbed in the water immediately. She used what strength she had to wave the hand to and fro in hopes that Miles or Burgle would see it.

Tears had frozen to her face. Time was running out.

Then, just before she lost all sensation in her fingers, she felt, ever so slightly . . . something.

Yes. Something had tugged on her hand.

Penelope pulled her numb hand from the water

as if it were no longer her own—and to her surprise, another hand was clasped to it. The weight beneath it felt more like a hundred-pound cinder block than a human being, and Penelope, though fierce and full of adrenaline, did not have the strength.

"Pull!" she ordered Teddy Bronconato.

Teddy yanked the rope as hard as he could. A few kids joined in. Then more. As they pulled, for a moment Penelope thought her leg might be separated from the rest of her body. But she did not let go of the hand clinging to her own.

Little by little, the children dragged her away from the hole, and a body emerged from the water, blue and gasping.

Miles.

He looked less distressed than disoriented and was tugging at his own leg. The children saw another hand wrapped around Miles's skate, its sausage-like fingers clutching the blade. Burgle's.

With a final burst of strength, the kids pulled Teddy Bronconato, who pulled Penelope, who was using every ounce of strength to pull Miles, who had somehow managed to pull Burgle.

Moments later, as Burgle and Miles lay on the sidelines, shaking and sopping wet, Penelope hugged her brother as hard as she ever had. Principal Flincher appeared with a couple of blankets and wrapped up the two shivering victims. Teddy draped his coat over Penelope's shoulders.

While she sat waving her fingers, starting to feel hints of a tingle in her pinkie and ring finger, Penelope saw Burgle's and Miles's chests heaving, their desperate breath steaming the air. And she knew they'd survive.

Some kids cried. Others clapped or hugged or patted each other on the back. They had all aided in the rescue.

All except one, that is. While Glacier Cove Academy's middle school was pulling together, and later weeping and rejoicing together, one child stood alone, her face blank and impassive, arms folded across her chest: Coral Wanamaker.

CHAPTER 11

News of the daring rescue on Lake Trenchfoot spread around Glacier Cove: How Penelope March, of all people, had saved the day with her quick thinking. How the big, dumb gym teacher, despite his bravery, had been dragged from the water by Miles March rather than the other way around. And how both of them had been rescued by a bunch of middle schoolers.

Penelope was asked to retell the story so many times that she began to add little flourishes here and there. ("My fingers felt like ten baby carrots in a pot of boiling water. . . .") Eventually she just nodded and smiled. People could fill in the rest with their imagination.

No one knew what exactly had happened under the ice. Well, Miles and Burgle did, but neither was saying much. Anyone courageous enough to visit the gym teacher in the intensive care wing of GC General, where a team of doctors attempted to treat his severe hypothermia, was greeted with the same response: "THANK YOU FOR VISITING. CAN YOU GET ME ANOTHER BLANKET, PLEASE?"

One day, Penelope and her father went to check on Miles, who was recovering from his own hypothermia two floors below Burgle. When they walked into Miles's room, they found him thrashing around under the bedcovers like a maniac.

"Good Lord," Russell March gasped, and bolted from the room to fetch a nurse. He was still a bit jumpy after all his children had been through.

The moment he was gone, Penelope lifted the blanket. Underneath, Miles had handcuffed himself to a bedpost and was struggling to pick the lock.

Penelope kissed her brother's cheek. "Feeling better, I see."

He sank back into the wrinkled sheets. "I've got to do something to keep busy."

"You that bored?"

"Well, let's see. While the nurse was changing my

bandages last night, she gave me the complete medical history of all nine of her cats. That was pretty exciting."

Penelope laughed. "I miss you, Miles."

Miles sank his teeth into his lower lip. His famous smile was gone. Wrinkles around his eyes made him look like a shriveled old man.

"I have a riddle," Penelope said. "What eleven-letter word does everyone pronounce incorrectly?"

Miles stared absently out the window at a flag flapping in the wind.

"Give up?"

He went back to work on the handcuffs. It was almost as though he hadn't heard.

"Incorrectly," Penelope said. "Get it?"

Before he could respond, the nurse darted in with Russell. "What's going on, child? Is everything all right? . . . Are those handcuffs?"

At the sight of Cat Lady Nurse, Penelope burst into laughter, which confused their father and angered the nurse, who demanded the key to the cuffs.

Penelope decided not to push Miles. He'd talk when he was ready. She stayed by her brother's side for the rest of the day, even after their father returned to work, and she read aloud from a book about volcano eruptions. Miles remained silent, his thoughts locked in a room somewhere far away that Penelope could not locate.

Buzzardstock was putting the finishing touches on a lovely sculpture of a monkey riding a unicycle when he heard the knock at his door. He ignored it. Then another knock, louder. He groaned and put down his chain saw. If it was the mailman needing an ice pick to get the mailbox open again . . .

When Buzzardstock opened the front door, he found Coral Wanamaker spitting a fingernail on his porch.

The girl cleared her throat. "Do you need an assistant?"

Buzzardstock raised his green eyebrows. "Well, now, I'm not—"

"I'm stronger than I look and I don't talk much."

"Be that as it may, I don't—"

"Great," Coral said. "I'll start tomorrow at three-thirty. We'll discuss payment later."

Before Buzzardstock could object, Coral turned and ran from the porch.

"What on earth was that?" Buzzardstock asked

Wolfknuckle after closing the door. But the dog was far more interested in his chew toy.

Three days later, the hospital discharged Miles. His frostbite had been mild and would heal within two weeks. Burgle had not been so lucky; two of his toes and one of his fingers had been so severely damaged that they were infected with gangrene. They would have to be amputated.

That night, just as Penelope started to drift off in her hammock, Miles sat up in his.

"Pen. There's something I need to tell you." He took a deep breath. "I saw . . . something . . . under the ice. Something I can't explain. It was our bedroom. The hammocks, the pillows, the lamp, everything. Then our house. Then the block, then the whole town. Glacier Cove was underwater, the cars and buildings, the entire library, books and all, floating underwater. People were drowning, reaching out for help. But I couldn't help. The whole town sank farther and farther, and then . . ."

Miles couldn't bring himself to say it out loud, but as he'd been underwater, gawking at the helpless people floating past him, a shadow emerged over everything. No, it was more than a shadow. It was as though someone had turned off a giant light, plunging the entire ocean into darkness so pure that Miles could not see his hand in front of his face. He'd felt a chill that went way beyond hypothermia, a dread that lodged itself in his heart and his hands and every other part of him, a low, moaning terror so deep and agonizing that all he wanted to do was sink to the bottom of the ocean and end it. That was the moment on Lake Trenchfoot when Penelope's hand found Miles's and pulled him from the blackness.

"Then what?" Penelope asked.

"Glacier Cove was gone."

Penelope shuddered. The wind screeched outside their bedroom window.

"I know it sounds weird," Miles said. "It was like a dream, but these things were right in front of me—I could touch them. Smell them. I saw the words in a book floating past! It felt so real. When you pulled me out of the water, I couldn't believe everyone was still there."

"What do you think it means?"

"I don't know. But I'm really scared."

"Did Burgle see anything underwater?"

"When I asked if he saw anything strange, he said, 'YEAH. I SAW MYSELF DROWNING.'"

Penelope laughed, and that made Miles laugh—with a surprised look on his face, as if he'd forgotten how good it felt. But then the laughter stopped and they fell into a thick silence. Penelope's mind drifted through possibilities about Glacier Cove, before landing squarely on one single, obvious thought: Buzzardstock.

CHAPTER 12

When he answered the door, the old man looked as though he hadn't slept in forty-eight hours. Or maybe forty-eight years. His matted green hair poked out in every direction. Saying he looked like a vampire was an insult to vampires.

Buzzardstock waved Penelope and Miles inside the gallery, which was a mess. Papers and tools were everywhere. The half-finished pieces around them had gotten even more twisted. Penelope's eyes landed on a sculpture of a drooling baby sleeping in a crib overflowing with scorpions. "Nightmare City, that one," Buzzardstock said. "I don't know what I was thinking."

Miles eyed Buzzardstock coldly. Penelope had

dragged him back to the Ice House, and he'd only agreed to go when she threatened to go alone. He didn't relish the thought of his sister alone with this crazy man and wanted to get in and out of the house as quickly as possible. Then he stopped.

Across the gallery was Coral, picking up tools off the floor. She nodded at Penelope.

"Coral?" Penelope said. She was somehow not surprised to see her there. The girl had a knack for showing up where you least expected it.

"My new assistant," Buzzardstock said. The old man leaned in conspiratorially. "Do either of you have any idea what a fair wage is for an assistant?"

"Ore9n," Penelope murmured. "I know you don't believe in privacy, but . . ." She motioned at Coral.

Buzzardstock nodded. "Very well. You're free to go, Miss Wanamaker, and my heartiest thanks for all your hard work today." He surveyed the chaos of his workspace. "The place looks great."

Coral grabbed her things and smiled her weird smile at Penelope.

Once Coral left, Penelope launched into the tale: the ice cracking, the rescue, the strange vision of Glacier Cove that Miles had seen while plunging under Lake Trenchfoot.

Buzzardstock listened in sullen silence. A black tabby house cat peeked around the pool table, fixing its almond-shaped eyes on Penelope for a moment in the judgmental way that cats do. When it slipped away, she noticed a little stump where its tail should have been.

Buzzardstock put his hand on Miles's shoulder. "You ate the dream cookie."

Miles looked away.

"You ate my cookie?" Penelope had assumed that she'd lost it on Lake Trenchfoot.

"I snuck it from your coat when you weren't looking."

"That was my cookie!"

Buzzardstock cleared his throat. "I don't wish to split hairs here, but you were never actually offered the cookie."

Penelope's outrage wilted into embarrassment. "Oh. Right. About that—"

"I'm sorry, Pen," said Miles. "Believe me, I wish I hadn't." His face hardened as he swiveled to face Buzzardstock. "So. Why did I see this whole town floating underwater?"

"Oh, dear. Those dream cookies—they are delectable, are they not? Something about the recipe tends to make unusual things happen. I think it's all the nutmeg. I put in four teaspoons and then mix—"

"What unusual things?" Miles interrupted.

"Well, some who eat a dream cookie see memories of their past. Others see wishes for the present. What you experienced, I fear, was something far worse."

"Which is?"

"A vision of the future."

"Okay, then," Miles said sarcastically, leaning over to Penelope. "Can we go now?"

"Tell me something," said Buzzardstock. "Did you hear a strange sound just before the ice cracked? A loud pop?"

"Yes."

"And a sort of fizzing?"

"We all heard it. How did you know?"

"I know ice," Buzzardstock said. "The sound you heard is called a Bergie Seltzer. It happens when the water-ice interface reaches compressed air bubbles that have been trapped in the ice. The bubbles contain air imprisoned in snow layers from early in the ice's history. Each bubble bursts, like a balloon. Pop! A Bergie Seltzer."

"Why does it happen?"

"It occurs when a large body of ice melts. The

density of pure ice is roughly 920 kilograms per cubic meter, but the density of sea water is 1,025 kilograms per cubic meter."

"What does that mean?"

"It means, my dear children, that something terrible is happening beneath our feet right now." Buzzardstock pulled a metallic gizmo from his lab coat and pushed a button.

A rumble emanated from the Ice House's walls, as if a giant machine's clanking gears had been activated. A rectangular opening appeared on the wall, revealing a small chamber lit in an eerie red glow from a shining chandelier made of tiny golf balls, Ping-Pong balls, yarn balls, and eyeballs.

"Are you ready?" Buzzardstock asked. Neither child had the slightest idea what it was they were supposed to be ready for. "Well? What are you waiting for? Has *neither* of you seen an iceslidevator before?"

Miles and Penelope looked at each other. *Don't,* Miles's eyes said.

Penelope, who had never considered herself the braver of the two, stepped forward, brushing past her brother and Buzzardstock. Miles hurried into the chamber, too, as if he preferred its unknown dangers to being alone with the old man. Inside, an array of buttons, little circles of neon just begging to be pushed, covered one wall. Penelope didn't dare.

"Hold on," said Buzzardstock, who was suddenly inside the iceslidevator with them.

He pushed a button and the door closed. The little room began to spin, slowly at first, then faster and faster, until the three of them were banging into walls like ice cubes in a blender.

Penelope screamed. Miles screamed.

But they were spiraling so fast it was impossible to tell whose screams were whose, so it all sounded like one terrible *AIIIEEOOOOGG!!* Just when Penelope thought she might pass out, the floor disappeared, sending the three of them tumbling down into darkness.

CHAPTER 13

Even in the dark, Penelope could make out the shape of the slide, which corkscrewed and doubled back on itself with geometric precision. At some point, even as her body picked up speed and hurtled forward with no clear destination, she got used to the ride. Just when she was starting to enjoy it— THOOMP!—Penelope dropped into a giant, dim chamber filled with sponge balls. Two more *thoomps* followed.

"Miles?" Penelope called. "You all right?"

Twenty feet away, Miles's body popped up over the surface of the sponge balls. "That was kind of fun."

"I trust everyone still has all their arms and legs?"

Buzzardstock asked, jumping to his feet with surprising agility. "Actually, at this point all you need are legs. Follow me."

The three of them entered a narrow tunnel, its walls lit by tiny lightbulbs encased in different-colored ice blocks. Penelope felt like she was walking on the inside of a kaleidoscope. A very, very cold kaleidoscope.

"Where are we?" she asked.

"Fifteen stories beneath my home," Buzzardstock murmured. "Inside the iceberg. The inner sanctum, as it were. This ridiculous hunk of frozen water upon which we reside is much deeper than you think. Glacier Cove is about five hundred feet above the ocean, but the ice beneath it descends nearly a mile underwater." Then he turned to the children, as if to emphasize the point he was about to make. "You've heard the phrase 'tip of the iceberg'? I'm afraid that's all our hometown is."

The tunnel led to an enormous purple room with a high ceiling. The room, a massive circle carved out of the ice, was empty but for one thing: a small marble slab resting on a pedestal in the center of the room.

"You go on ahead," said Buzzardstock. The old

man's brow furrowed into an apprehensive expression that Penelope hadn't seen before. His feet made it clear that they would carry him no closer.

As Miles and Penelope studied the strange slab, both felt a new fear wash over them. Each knew, somehow, that something terrible had happened in this very spot, and not so long ago. Yet both were drawn to the slab, approaching it as if pulled by an imaginary force. Their hands found each other and gripped tight as they crept closer.

"Want to hear something funny?" Miles mumbled. "The cookie wasn't even that good."

"Go ahead, touch it," Buzzardstock whispered. "Really, it's harmless."

"Then why aren't you coming?"

Miles and Penelope gaped at the slab. She squeezed his hand. "You first."

"No, you."

"How about together?"

"No. You."

Penelope let go of her brother's hand and ran her fingers along the slab's surface. It felt like ordinary marble, cold and smooth and vaguely otherworldly.

When Miles saw that nothing catastrophic had befallen his sister, he touched the slab, too, which made his cold fingers tingle. Then he noticed a strange slot on its side. "What's this?"

"Smart boy," Buzzardstock said. From the across the room, the old man pulled the metallic gizmo from his pocket, inserted a key, and turned it.

The slab slid open, revealing a curved compartment in the center scarcely large enough to slide a hand into. "That, my children, is where I keep . . . the Shard," Buzzardstock said. "The last remaining piece of Makara Nyx's fortress. The only thing that keeps her from withering away and dying. Passed down from my father, tracing back through seven generations of Buzzardstock guardians. And just maybe the reason Glacier Cove has survived all these years."

"But it's empty," said Miles.

"Yes, there's the dilemma. It wasn't empty two days ago."

"So where is it?"

Buzzardstock rubbed his mole and looked at the floor. He had no idea.

"Wait," Penelope said, her blood running cold. "Makara Nyx was here?"

"Until yesterday, I had my doubts. But now . . ." His voice trailed off. "Frankly, I'm not sure how she got in or how she knew it was here. But unless someone finds this evil beast and gets the Shard back, the ice that broke on Lake Trenchfoot is only the beginning."

After a trip back through the kaleidoscope tunnel, onto the corkscrewing slides that somehow launched them upward as though gravity were working in reverse, and then another white-knuckle screamfest in the iceslidevator, the three of them were back in Buzzardstock's gallery. But to Penelope, everything felt different.

CHAPTER 14

Around that time, strange things began to happen in Glacier Cove.

First, scores of residents reported seeing bizarre, jellyfish-like clouds in the sky. The town's UFO believers went bonkers, swearing they had heard a strange language coming from each cloud.

GC Academy's science teacher explained that the cloud phenomenon was called *virga*. "It happens when ice crystals in clouds fall but evaporate before hitting the ground," he said. "It's pretty rare around here, but it's possible the same thing happens in space. So maybe the kooks are on to something."

A construction worker named Leonard Pogue reported an avalanche on the north side when he came home from work to find a seventy-foot mountain of snow where his house once stood. A shrewd man, Pogue built an enormous igloo and opened Pogue's Cone Zone, a successful snow-cone stand. So the Pogues managed just fine, thank you very much.

Then there was that business at the GC Municipal Jail. When none of the twenty-four prisoners appeared at breakfast one morning, guards rushed to the prisoners' cells and found two surprises. The first was that the inmates were gone. The second was that all twenty-four cells were flooded knee-deep with stagnant water pouring in through a gap where the wall met the floor.

"The adverse weather must have caused the prison's eastern wall to erode at the base, which provided the inmates in cell block nine just enough space to squeeze under," the warden told a reporter from the *Daily Icicle*. "They swam to freedom. That's the only possibility. Trust me, these chowderheads weren't smart enough to escape on their own."

Next, the crabeater seals disappeared from the zoo. Echoing the prison escape, the seals swam from their enclosure and never looked back. The prison was on the west side of town, and the escapees went east. The zoo was on the east side, and the seals traveled west. Periodically, an escaped prisoner would pass an escaped seal, and each would nod quietly at the other and keep moving so as not to arouse suspicion.

It must be reported here that the residents did not seem terribly troubled by these occurrences. Quite the opposite, actually. As the sun emerged from behind its usual wall of clouds and the town thawed, so did people's cautions. Instead of fretting over, say, the fact that McCallister's Butcher Shop was under three feet of water, and the sausages that poor McCallister had been curing since Lord Knows When were now floating around the shop like delicious but doomed canoes, Glacier Covians were flinging off their clothes and jumping, pasty white skin and all, into the many small lakes now populating the landscape. The whole town was outside. School was canceled for a day, if only because the superintendent didn't know what else to do.

Most everyone assumed these were odd coincidences, the kind of things that *just happen*, but Penelope knew. The water *drip-drip-drip*ping from icicles, the giant puddles forming everywhere, the periodic pop and sizzle rumbling underground. It all added up to one undeniable fact that no one else would acknowledge.

Glacier Cove was melting.

Penelope's concern for her brother doubled. He seemed to be melting too. Not *actually* melting, of course, but since the accident and the experience at Buzzardstock's, he'd grown more withdrawn and morose. His smile had been replaced with a dead-eyed look that chilled Penelope to the core.

"What are we going to do?" she asked him one day.

"About what?"

"The Shard. Glacier Cove. You."

Miles scoffed. "Jeez, stop with the drama."

"Wait. You don't believe Buzzardstock?"

"Come on, Pen. The old man is crazier than a cross-eyed caribou."

Again, Penelope heard Stella Wanamaker's raspy voice: *A stranger has entered your life. Do not trust this stranger.*

"Sure, Ore9n's a little odd," Penelope said. "But he doesn't seem crazy."

"Which makes more sense? That an ancient shape-shifting sea goddess snuck under his house to steal a magic crystal so she could melt the town or that Buzzardstock is a creepy old man with a chain saw and too much time on his hands?"

"But . . . why would he make it all up?"

"I don't know," Miles said. "Maybe he enjoys scaring kids."

"What about, you know . . . what you saw underwater? Was that real?"

"I don't know what it was. Look, you're the only person I care about in this whole town. Dad, sometimes. And I'm telling you. Stay away from Ore9n Buzzardstock. The man is going to do nothing but get us into trouble."

Penelope had always assumed that her brother liked trouble.

What she didn't know was that Miles had been having horrible nightmares since he'd eaten Buzzardstock's dream cookie. It started with the usual stuff. He dreamed he was late for school and couldn't find his classroom, or he was falling into an endless black hole. But then the dreams got worse. He was trapped in a dark closet, the walls closing in until they threatened to crush him, or his teeth crumbled in his mouth and sifted to the ground in a fine powder.

Each dream plunged his mind into a gloomy netherworld that cut deep into his fears. When the nightmares assumed no definable shape beyond the same raw terror he'd felt under Lake Trenchfoot,

Miles began to dread the night altogether. He tried to just ignore the problem and hope it went away. As with any problem larger than a headache, it didn't. So Miles downed a few cups of his father's turnip coffee in hopes of keeping awake. When that didn't work, he pinched his skin. Eventually, his eyes grew heavy and he dozed off, and the whole thing started over.

Miles had lost so much weight that he poked four new holes on his belt with a pen, and the fantastical visions that haunted his dreams spilled over into his waking hours. In Escapology Club, he felt something wiggling in his straitjacket and thought he saw a big hairy spider—*No! Two spiders!*—scurrying up his neck. He nearly tore the straitjacket apart trying to get out.

The other member of the Escapology Club quit after that. "Man, Miles has been weird since he fell through that ice," he told another kid. "I think he's losing it."

"I'd say he lost it," said the other kid.

The final straw came during math class, when Miles saw the chalkboard open up and a tidal wave of frigid saltwater gush out. He screamed until the water filled his lungs; then he closed his eyes and gave in to the rush of water. When he opened them, the water was gone and his classmates were working on a math problem on the chalkboard. And Miles was sitting at his desk, bone dry and coughing.

He had spent much of the past few months escaping from chains and boxes, but he had no idea how to wiggle his way out of this torture. He had to do something. Only two solutions made any sense. One was to never sleep again. The other was even scarier.

Miles poked his head in the creaky door of Wanamaker's Fortune-Telling Emporium. From across the room, Stella Wanamaker saw the terrified-looking boy in her doorway.

"Come, come," she said. "Or go, go. You're letting the cold air in."

Vaguely nauseated by the smell of wax and bird feathers, Miles took a tentative step inside. The door closed behind him with a dull thud. "Hi," he said, trying to sound chipper. "I'm—"

"Silence." The old lady approached him. "Do not say a thing. Who you are. Why you're here. Your problem. I will find problem. Remove your coat." She put her cold hand on his back, sharp fingernails digging into his shoulder. "Would you like a cup of *schlerguth*? Good for digestion."

Miles shook his head. He didn't know what *schlerguth* was—some kind of gross tea, maybe—but he was fairly certain that he did not want it. The bird squawked from the corner, as if to say *Good call. Avoid the schlerguth.*

Stella ushered Miles to a wobbly table, nudged him into an unstable chair, and reached behind the counter to grab her candles and bowl. "Many ways to tell fortune," she said. "All *rubbish*, for fools and by fools. Except one. Place candles in bowl."

Miles took the candles, one red and one black, and stood them in the brass bowl. Stella watched closely with her one good eye and almost smiled. She took the bowl and placed it on an oven burner.

A flame immediately shot out of the bowl—one giant, angry flare that seemed to cut the air over the stove in half. Then it disappeared so quickly Miles wasn't even sure it was real.

It was real. Stella jumped back, the fire just missing her cheek. But it had not missed her completely—it had seared off her tarantula eyebrows. The stench of burning hair lent an extra layer of ick to the room.

Unfazed, Stella peered back into the bowl. Without eyebrows, her face appeared to be in a constant state of surprise. "Come closer," she said.

Miles got up from the table. He considered running out the door; instead he teetered to the stove. In the bowl, the candles had burned down to one goopy layer of purple.

"Tell me, child, what do you see?"

"Wax."

"Look harder."

"But I'm not a fortune-teller."

Stella clucked her tongue. "You see more of the future than I."

"Why do you say that?"

"Because"—she pointed at the stove—"I did not even turn on the burner yet. So tell me. What do you see?"

Miles felt a weird quiver. He studied the wax and then closed his eyes. A series of images appeared, each quick and sharp. Some were fuzzy, as if viewed through a screen door, others clear as water. A cookie . . . a pile of broken pencils . . . a ticking watch . . . three penguins who almost seemed to be smiling . . . a submarine . . . bowls stacked in a cupboard . . . a volcano . . . flapping orange tubeworms on the side of a mountain . . . an icy tire swing hanging from a tree . . . Stella Wanamaker laughing—

Disoriented, Miles's eyes shot open. The wax in the

bowl had hardened, and so had his confusion. Now he had Stella Wanamaker smiling at him curiously.

"Tell me. What promises does your future make?"

Miles backed away. "I gotta go."

"What is your name, child?"

Miles grabbed his coat.

"*Stop*," Stella said.

Miles did not stop. Before he could even get his coat on, he was out the door and running down the street, more horrified than before.

"Forget payment!" Stella's laughing voice called after him. "Pay you, I should!"

CHAPTER 15

While the ginger-toned sun cast a heavy shade over the west side, Penelope trudged across the tundra's slushy slopes and ever-widening crevasses. At one point, a fugitive crabeater seal slid past her on the icy sidewalk, covering its sheepish face with a fin.

Penelope's destination was the Grotto, a hidden cave accessible to anyone small enough to squeeze through the small jagged opening on the side of an ice peak. Kids had turned it into a clubhouse of sorts; Penelope heard that high schoolers used the space on weekends for turnip-beer keg parties. After a lengthy search, she found the opening and shimmied inside.

As she stomped and shook the ice off herself, Penelope's eyes adjusted to the dim light. Then all at once she stopped. Her blood didn't just go cold. It stopped pumping through her veins entirely.

Someone was standing in the corner.

"Who's there?" Penelope's voice echoed off the rocky walls.

The body stepped into the light, or what little light had filtered into the cave. Before Penelope could even make out the face, she saw the black clothes and knew. It was Coral Wanamaker.

"Jeez, Coral! You scared me! What are you doing?"

Coral considered the question and jammed her hands in her pockets. "Followed you."

"But you got here before I did."

Coral made a face that could have qualified as a smile or a grimace or even an itchy nose, and the girls sank into an awkward silence. The only noise came from a petrel scavenging for food, its yellow bird feet *scritch-scritch-scritch*ing against the ice. Coral spied a deck of cards on the ice coffee table. "Wanna play gin rummy?"

The two girls sat on the makeshift ice couch, their feet on the coffee table. As they played cards, shadows from a crackling bonfire flashed on the sky-high ceiling. The petrel lay on its belly at their feet like a dog too lazy to go outside.

"Why did you take the job at Buzzardstock's?" Penelope asked.

Coral looked away. "Honestly? To get out of my house. Stella's a little hard to be around right now."

"What do you mean?"

"She's becoming . . . oh, I don't know. Can we talk about literally anything else?"

"Fine. Do you believe Buzzardstock's story?"

Coral seemed equally uncomfortable with this subject. She put down her cards to bite her thumbnail. "Which part?"

"The whole thing."

"You first," said Coral.

"I asked you first."

"So?"

Penelope thought for a moment. "What if we both write it down on a piece of paper, like a secret ballot, and then we hand our ballot to each other at the same time?"

"That's fair."

Penelope reached into her backpack for two pencils and tore off two scraps of paper. She handed one to Coral. A moment later, each girl had folded her paper and placed it on the coffee table. But just as they were reaching for the scraps, the petrel nabbed both wads in its beak and flew out through the Grotto's opening.

The girls laughed so hard their glee bounced off the walls of the cave, until it sounded like an entire auditorium of children laughing. Soon they forgot Buzzardstock and made their way back to town.

The bird didn't make it far before spitting out its meal. If, through some weird twist of events, someone had happened to be standing outside the Grotto at the exact moment the petrel came shooting out, he would have seen its body twist in midair and expand into something purple and repulsive, full of teeth and tentacles and oozing sores, before morphing into a small fish and plopping into the water. If that person had not been puzzled and petrified by such a sight and decided to descend into a deep crevasse twenty yards from the opening of the Grotto, he would've found two wadded-up scraps of paper. On one scrap, he would find three mysterious words written in loopy cursive:

I believe him.

The other would be blank.

That night, long after Miles had thrashed his way into a troubled sleep, Penelope hopped from her hammock to get a drink of water. She tiptoed across the floor, trying to avoid the creaky floorboards, and peeked into the kitchen.

Her father sat at his usual spot with his usual glass, his back to Penelope. A nearly empty bottle was on the table in front of him.

As if sensing her presence, her father turned around. "What're you doing up?" he slurred. His eyes were bloodshot, his face a mess.

"I'll go back to bed," Penelope said quickly.

"No," he said, patting the empty chair beside him. "Sit down."

Penelope sized up the situation. A photo album sat on his lap, a big brown leather book that had been perused so often the pictures were falling out. She didn't like to be around her father when he was drinking, but he looked so lonely.

In fairness, Russell March could be a gentleman and a gentle man. When the kids were little, he used to sing them to sleep with made-up lullabies: *"Geese and ducks and owls and parrots / eat bugs and twigs and moldy carrots / and sing with cows and naked sheep / and fall into a slumber deep. . . ."* At some point the lullabies stopped, but more than once, Penelope woke to find her father caressing her hair with his coarse fingers and with a bittersweet smile on his face. It was the best feeling on earth. Those were the good nights.

Penelope sat down and they flipped through the album, perusing the faces of old family members. Large groups of grim-faced ancestors posing in thick wool coats in a dusty parlor. A delighted toddler on shaky legs with her arms wrapped around an unopened present. A ruddy-faced man on a rickety ladder cleaning out the gutters of an old house.

"Is it true that Uncle Murph had eleven toes?" Penelope asked.

"Where'd you hear that?"

"Miles swears it's true."

"Uncle Murph did *not* have eleven toes."

"Really?"

"Really. Uncle Murph had twelve toes."

They came to a photo of a beautiful, delicate woman with brown eyes and dark wavy hair. She was sitting cross-legged on the snowy roof of a car that had been laid out with a picnic, her face frozen in a crooked smile radiating love and mischief and a vague sadness.

Penelope had seen this photo before, and every time she saw it, the crooked smile hurt a little more. It was as though this woman—who Penelope knew to be her mother even though her father would never say so—could read what was in Penelope's heart and liked what she found there, but was also somehow disappointed.

The two of them stared at it, studying her smile and thinking how easily life could have been different. Each seemed to be waiting for the other to speak.

For a quick moment, Penelope wanted to tell her father about Buzzardstock and Makara Nyx and the Shard. She wanted to tell him how scared she was. She wanted to tell him she knew she was different from everyone else and felt a constant, nagging *ache* for something she could not identify. But she didn't know where to begin.

The moment passed. Her father flashed a half-hearted grin and closed the book. "C'mon," he said in a hollow voice, patting Penelope's leg with as much rough tenderness as he could muster. "I'll tuck you in."

CHAPTER 16

After a brief burst of goodwill due to the Lake Trenchfoot rescue, Penelope found many of her classmates even crueler than before.

Many of the taunts now revolved around Mr. Stingleberry, who could not hide his gushy awe at Penelope's ingenuity on Lake Trenchfoot. He made a big embarrassing deal of calling on her constantly, even when she didn't have her hand up. Once, he brought a camera and asked a kid to take a picture of him and Penelope for his daughter. The others, of course, jumped on that delicious opportunity.

"Penelope and Stingleberry sitting in a tree," one of the Funkhausers chanted in the lunchroom.

"*K-I-S-I* . . . um . . . *K-I-S-T* . . . Gerhard, how do you spell *kissing*?"

"*S-T-U-P-I-D*," the other twin answered, before bopping his brother on the head with his meaty fist. "Hey, Smell-O-Pee. When Stingleberry's kissing you and he hiccups, can you taste his lunch?"

There were exceptions to the unpleasantness, of course. Lilith Wimberley sometimes sat with her and Coral at lunch. And Teddy Bronconato showed his respect by punching the arm of anyone who bad-mouthed Penelope. Not that he ever talked to her.

One day, Penelope decided to use her teacher's admiration to her advantage. After all the other students had left, she milled about in the back of the classroom while Mr. Stingleberry tidied up his desk.

"Penelope March!" he said, as if addressing a celebrity rather than a sixth grader. "Shouldn't you be off performing heroic acts of—*HIC!*—great daring?"

"Mr. Stingleberry, I have a problem."

"Only one? I've got thousands." He chuckled at his joke until he saw that Penelope was dead serious. "I'm sorry. What's up?"

"Do you know Ore9n Buzzardstock?"

Stingleberry's smile faded. The name seemed to

affect his posture, which deflated until he looked less like a man and more like a saggy sack of potatoes.

"Is he crazy?" Penelope asked.

"I'd rather not . . ." Stingleberry seemed prepared to say more. Instead he inhaled deeply in hopes of warding off any fear and potential hiccups that might follow.

Penelope noticed his hands were shaking. She wouldn't have been surprised if he burst into tears. But she couldn't stop now. "Do you trust him? Because I was at his house, and he told me some strange things—"

"All right, that's enough—"

"—and I'm not entirely certain—"

"Enough!" Stingleberry said so loudly that Penelope felt his breath on her face. "That . . . man . . . is a danger to himself and to others!"

"Why?"

His eyes blazing with distress, the teacher grabbed Penelope's hands. "You must make me a promise, Penelope March. Do not go back inside that house."

"But why is he a danger—"

"*Promise!*" Stingleberry stomped his foot with such force that a framed picture of a snowman fell from the wall and shattered.

Penelope had never seen a grown man so out of control. His sweaty hands wrapped around hers so tightly that her fingers began to go numb.

"Fine. I promise."

"Good. That's good." Stingleberry released Penelope's hands. He glanced at his wrist, though his watch was on the other arm, then stuffed a crumpled heap of papers into his bag while leaving others on his desk. "Right now, I find myself—*HURP*—late for a pressing appointment. One that cannot be missed. Goodbye."

"Wait! Mr. Stingleberry—"

Within seconds, her teacher was out the door and gone, leaving Penelope alone with a large pile of broken glass and an even larger pile of questions.

Penelope didn't know what, or who, to believe. She wanted nothing more than to be in the Ice House with a flashlight and a magnifying glass, searching for clues that would lead her to Makara Nyx.

Instead, she found herself hiding behind a garbage can on South Cloudburst Avenue. Her father had forced her outside to play with the neighborhood kids, who were embroiled in what was supposed to be an epic water balloon fight.

It turned out to be less fun than expected. Penelope had filled her first balloon too full and watched it slip from her hands and break on the ground. Then she didn't fill the second enough, so when she threw it at a very surprised Stewart Peck, point-blank, instead of soaking him it bounced off and burst on the concrete. Either way, nothing much was getting wet other than the ground. But the kids still hooted and hollered, like a water balloon fight where no one got wet was the greatest game ever.

As Penelope crouched behind the garbage can, third balloon in hand, this one filled just right, Buzzardstock's words to Miles echoed in her head like the sound of a professor rehearsing in an empty classroom:

"Some who eat a dream cookie see memories of their past. Others see wishes for the present. What you experienced, I fear, was something far worse . . . a vision of the future."

She replayed the ominous words Miles said to her as they were falling asleep the night before:

"Yes, I'm seeing things. But it's not the future. It's just random, terrible things. And I want it to all go away."

Splat!

A balloon exploded on the back of Penelope's

113

head with such force she dropped her own balloon, which of course popped and poured out onto the ground. She felt cold water running down her back.

"Got you!" Stewart Peck ran off cackling. "I got Smell-O-Pee!"

Some of the other kids high-fived him, while others hurled balloons of their own, missing him left and right and high and low. Penelope shook her hair, spraying water in all directions, and went off in search of a towel. She'd had enough.

Buzzardstock was already standing in his doorway when she arrived. "Where's your brother?" he asked, less curious than playful.

"He thinks there's something wrong with you."

"Of course there is. The point being?"

"Ore9n, may I ask you something?"

"Please, come in—"

"Do you know a man named Paul Stingleberry?"

"Hmm." Buzzardstock looked up at the skies, pretending he didn't remember, though he obviously did. "Why do you ask?"

"He's my teacher. When I mentioned your name, he flipped out."

Buzzardstock chuckled to himself. "Yes, that

sounds about right. Of course I know Paul. Or rather, I knew him. Paul Stingleberry was my protégé many years ago. He was interested in learning the art, and he showed a modest amount of skill, but ultimately we parted ways."

"Art? What art?"

"Ice sculpture, of course. Is there any other kind?"

"Did he quit?"

Buzzardstock raised his bushy green eyebrows. "There was . . . an accident. I'd rather not get into what happened, but . . . it happened. And nothing can change it. Suffice it to say, Paul suffered greatly afterward. Tell me, does he still hiccup?"

Penelope nodded.

"Yes, well, in the ensuing years, Paul thought I was off my rocker too," Buzzardstock said. "Rather than get the help he needed, he spent his time attempting to convince the authorities to lock me away in the mental ward at GC Hospital. I got countless visits from authority figures who asked the same questions over and over until they all concluded the same thing: that I was indeed a strange creature, but a harmless one."

Suddenly Buzzardstock looked vulnerable—just a fragile and misunderstood man—and Penelope felt silly for imagining he could be even remotely threatening.

"I think," she said, "that I would like a cookie and a cup of jasmine tea, please."

"A cookie?" Buzzardstock studied Penelope's face. "You do realize what could happen?"

"I do. And let's skip the tea."

Buzzardstock smiled. "Very well, then. One dream cookie, coming right up, for the one person in Glacier Cove who doesn't think I'm crazy."

CHAPTER 17

At first, Penelope felt nothing.

She wasn't sure what to expect. But as she wiped the cookie crumbs from her mouth, Penelope lay down in the loft overlooking Buzzardstock's gallery and felt pangs of guilt about how she had lied to Miles— *I have a homework project at Lilith Wimberley's*—and how quickly she had broken her promise to Stingleberry. This was more important than truth and promises, though. The sound of a dripping faucet from somewhere in Buzzardstock's home was a slow drumbeat echoing her lie.

Down below, Ore9n, having left Penelope alone (*"Trust me, it's far better if I'm not here to influence the experience"*), fired up his chain saw and worked on his latest piece, a three-tiered wedding cake made entirely of icy chicken feathers.

Soon the *ploop-ploop* of the faucet and the chain saw's rowdy buzz faded into each other, and the thoughts in Penelope's head began to jump from subject to subject without warning.

A popping campfire . . . the tangy smell of sweat during a footrace she had won in second grade . . . a red and white polka-dotted parachute puffing in the wind . . . then stalks of wheat and sewing machines and jangling keys, schools of mermaids blowing rainbow bubbles, a dusty box filled with shoes in a pristine field of snow-sprinkled poppies: each image danced past, flashing and folding into a blur until she wasn't certain whether these impressions were real or imagined. Then she was falling into the darkness until she found herself in the enormous purple room far beneath Buzzardstock's house.

At the sight of the empty marble slab in the middle of the room, Penelope felt a crippling dread. Why was she here? What was she meant to see? As she looked around the room for any kind of clue, something peculiar appeared on the floor.

Footprints.

Paw prints, actually, and small ones, each toepad

delicate and teardrop-shaped. Penelope crept alongside them, her heart pounding. The prints led to the slab, circled it, then led away from it in the other direction.

But the prints leading away were noticeably smaller, like those of a different animal. Something with lots of legs that scurried toward the far wall before disappearing.

Where— How—

She knelt where the prints faded into nothing and ran her hands along the wall. A few inches off the ground, her index finger found a hole so tiny that she almost didn't notice the pinprick of light shining through it.

Penelope stuck her finger in the hole and a tiny stream of cold water shot out. She plugged the hole with her thumb and the water stopped. When she pulled her thumb away, the stream surged once again. She pushed the hole ever so gently, and a small chunk of wall fell to the ground.

Penelope stared at the wall, and the water pouring from it, for what seemed like a few seconds. But it must have been longer, because the truth of what had happened hit her all at once, and she found herself back upstairs in Buzzardstock's loft, being sniffed by

Wolfknuckle, with no recollection of how she'd gotten there.

The jasmine tea she'd turned down before now felt good going down her throat, but not as good as the soft blanket Buzzardstock had slipped over her. The man could not hide his anxiety, pacing back and forth while Penelope described what she'd seen in the purple room.

"I hate to interrupt," Buzzardstock said, "but I must ask. Were they human footprints?"

"I don't think so."

Buzzardstock regarded his dog.

Wolfknuckle lifted his paws. *Don't look at me, old man.*

"The last time I was here," Penelope said, "I saw a cat with no tail wandering around."

"Majestica Jones," Buzzardstock said. Wolfknuckle began barking furiously at the mention of the name. "Well, that's what I call her, anyway. I rather like her company. She's a bit cantankerous, but no more so than any other cat. Doesn't much get along with my dog—hush, dog!—but she minds her own business."

"Where did you get her?"

"She simply appeared at my front door one day and started hanging around. I set out some milk every now and then, and she comes and goes as she pleases."

"Have you seen her lately?"

"No, not since—" Buzzardstock stopped. "Oh, good Lord. You don't think . . . ?"

"Makara Nyx is a shape-shifter, right? She can turn herself into anything."

Buzzardstock slapped his forehead. "Gadzooks, the cat!"

"She must have grabbed the Shard, turned herself into a spider or a ladybug or something, and somehow squeezed through the wall with it."

"The purest of evil was right under my nose! And I fed it skim milk!"

"Ore9n. What's on the other side of that wall?"

With that, Buzzardstock's face turned so pale that he looked like he might throw up. But instead of partially digested lunch, he spat out two words, and they were far worse.

"An ocean."

CHAPTER 18

The jagged shadows on Penelope's bedroom wall haunted her that night. Every icicle outside her window had melted into a strange shape, conspiring with the moonlight to project gnashing teeth and snarling lips on her wall.

For the first time ever, Miles had insisted on sleeping with the window open, causing the curtain to whip and flap about in the wind. More than anything, Penelope wanted to close the window, but she was too scared.

When she saw her brother fast asleep with the pillow over his face rising and falling with each breath— his fists clenched into little balls—Penelope had never felt so alone. She had not told him anything about her strange day, which almost made it seem like it hadn't happened.

She couldn't sleep. Buzzardstock's parting words on his doorstep had attached themselves to her brain and would not let go.

"It's you. You have a gift. Your brother has it, too, apparently. Both of you can see and experience things the rest of us can't. Take Stingleberry. Poor sap ate a dozen dream cookies in one sitting and never experienced anything other than indigestion. You, though? You're special. And you have a choice: you can run away from that gift—as your brother has done—or you can use it in the most valuable way. Which will you choose?"

The wind stopped moaning long enough for the room to grow still, but each time Penelope closed her eyes, the flapping curtain forced them open. She finally dropped off into the kind of sleep that feels less like rest and more like punishment.

And though no one was awake to see it, the shadows disappeared. The entire bedroom wall went black as something passed in front of the window. Whatever the something was, it was large enough to block out the moonlight pouring into the room.

It stopped and hovered, as if looking in the little window at the two sleeping children, sizing them up for something. Then it reached, with what looked like a long and bony claw, into the window, slowly enough that one could hear the wind whistling between its talons.

Penelope jerked awake in her hammock. Her whole body dripped with sweat and stiffened with fear at something she could not explain, something so real her teeth ached. But when she finally collected enough bravery to look out the window, she saw nothing but moonlight, shining through the curtain like a silvery spotlight.

CHAPTER 19

Wolfknuckle chewed the frayed strap of Penelope's backpack and watched her chisel an enormous block of ice. After three weeks of chipping away, it still looked to Penelope—and to Wolfknuckle—like an enormous block of ice. For all the hours the girl had spent at the Ice House, she had made very little progress.

At first, Penelope had come on weekends, telling her father that she was at Coral's. Then she began showing up at Buzzardstock's after school, and soon during lunch and recess. Sometimes she walked with Miles to school, watched him go in, then turned around and ran straight to the Ice House. Miles had wrapped himself too tightly in his own misery to notice. Stingleberry, between hiccups, had noted her absences, but he never said a word.

Penelope had begun determined and confident, assuming that Buzzardstock would have a plan to save Glacier Cove. If he did, he wasn't sharing it. The old man never once brought up Makara Nyx, nor did he mention the dream cookies or the vision Penelope had experienced. "Come this way," he'd said instead, and led her through the mazelike house to a closed door in back.

COLD ROOM, read the sign on the door. It opened to a cavernous and frigid workspace that was empty but for the previously mentioned enormous block of ice, two jumbo cooling fans, and a workbench full of tools.

As the two of them stood there admiring this blunt mass, Buzzardstock handed Penelope a chisel. "And now," he said, "you learn the lost art of ice sculpture."

Penelope tried to hand the chisel back. "You're kidding."

"I don't kid about ice sculpture."

"But why—"

The old man held up a wrinkly hand. "It's the only way."

"The only way to what?"

"Enough questions," Buzzardstock fired back. "You'll learn as you go. You must enter into this with a clear mind, or not at all. Now, loosen your grip. Treat the chisel like an extension of your hand. . . ."

Penelope learned her teacher's unusual approach to safety. If the old man remembered that his new protégée was only twelve, he gave no indication. Within days, he'd had her operating a blowtorch—*a blowtorch!*—and a chain saw. "I've modified the saw by removing some of the safety features from the cutting chains," Buzzardstock said. "Now, when I say go, you're going to plunge the tip into the ice. Beware the kickback, my dear. Goggles and earphones on. Go!"

And so the two of them spent hour after hour, week after week in the coldest room in Glacier Cove, Penelope training with the chisel, the chain saw, the various drills and bits and handsaws, none of which felt right in her hands as she chipped away at this impenetrable mass. Her muscles throbbed. The blisters on her hands had their own blisters. And her sunny optimism had shrunk to nothing.

This went on for some time. The vague answers, the lectures, the painstaking work with little headway. She didn't even know what she was supposed to be making or if she was making anything at all. But she kept showing up, trusting that Buzzardstock had some concrete goal in mind. Besides, it was better than school.

Coral Wanamaker was also a regular at the Ice House. But if she was still Buzzardstock's assistant, the job consisted mostly of checking on Penelope's progress and expressing how pointless it all was. "Wow, it looks just like it did last week," she said. "What is it, a giant loaf of bread with a toothpick stuck in it?"

Still, Penelope looked forward to Coral's visits. The girl could be wickedly funny, her tongue the lit fuse of a firecracker that she threw at any number of targets, including school ("Of course I hate it. Don't you?"), boys in their class ("bunch of sweaty tundra bozos"), Glacier Cove ("a rock of sludgy misery"), and Stingleberry ("a flopsweat freak show with the backbone of a marshmallow pie").

Today, though, Penelope's only company was Wolfknuckle. The dog's slurpy interest in her backpack strap increased in volume until Penelope could take it no longer. "Stop," she said, shooing Wolfknuckle away. The dog sauntered off in search of something else to chew.

There wasn't much to choose from. Outside the

Cold Room, the Ice House was disappearing before their eyes, its once-thick walls and roof thinning dangerously. Several staircases had vanished. Far worse, many of Buzzardstock's sculptures had melted into grotesque lumps. The smaller ones were now watery pools.

When Penelope opened the door of the Cold Room to let the dog out, she found Buzzardstock soaking up a puddle in the hallway with a towel. "I knew this day would come," he said. "I prepared myself for it, but I had no idea how terrible it would feel."

"Is it possible that no one notices we're living on a giant iceberg?" Penelope asked later as they worked on the block of ice together. "How do they not see it?"

"Oh, they know we're on an iceberg," Buzzardstock said. "They just don't care. Hand me that angle grinder, would you, my dear? Look. In Glacier Cove, people see what's easiest to see. They accept things as they are and don't ask questions. You, on the other hand, are curious. Try the ice pick for that edge there. You want to chip it away. No, like this." He took the pick from her hands and stabbed the ice, spraying icy sparks. "Try again."

"Maybe it would help if I knew what we were making."

"You want to know what we are making? We are making an education: yours. Now back to work."

One rainy afternoon, as Penelope was trying to smooth out a rough corner of the ice, the chisel slipped. A giant chunk of ice crumbled away.

"Stupid ice!" she screamed, and threw the chisel to the ground.

Buzzardstock exploded. "That is no way to treat my tools, you churlish little urchin!"

"I don't have to be here!" Penelope howled.

"So why *are* you here? If you find this all so distasteful?"

"I thought I was here to find the Shard! To help save this town!"

"No! You are here because you are lonely. Pour that emotion into the ice."

"It's just a bunch of frozen water."

Buzzardstock took a deep breath and smoothed out his eyebrows. "I'm going to pretend you didn't say that. Sit."

Penelope sat.

"My mother died when I was six," Buzzardstock began. "My father was so focused on his sculpture that he didn't notice me. When he spoke, it was usually to remind me how much of a distraction I was from his art. And he was an amazing artist. The way he treated the ice, with such tenderness—he certainly loved ice more than he loved people. Which is great if you're an art collector, but not great if you're related to the man.

"I learned the only way to get my father's attention was to follow in his footsteps. I found that ice sculpture fit my personality. The precision. The attention to detail. The endless possibilities. All locked in a simple, cold block. No matter how talented I got, though, nothing was enough for my father. There was no pride. No happiness. No nothing. Just work. The less he said, the harder I worked. By sixteen, I had given up any kind of social life."

"So why did you do it?"

"One day, I finished a complicated piece and it was the best work I had ever done. As I was standing there admiring it, I felt a hand on my back. It was my father. He squeezed my shoulder and nodded. Then he walked away. That was it: a squeeze and a nod. The only two compliments he ever paid me.

"It was the proudest moment of my life. The saddest too. Because I knew that although he was a great artist, he was a worthless parent. And if I wanted to follow in his footsteps as an artist, I would only end up doing the same as a father. Make a mistake with a block of ice? There is always another. But a child? So. I put my faith, my love—my everything—into the ice. Ice is enough for me. You have more in your life, and that gives you the potential to achieve so much more than I ever have. You're destined for bigger things."

Penelope wiped her eyes. "My mother died too. I wasn't even two."

Buzzardstock lowered his head. "I remember when it happened."

Penelope perked up. "What do you remember?"

"Very little, I'm afraid. I didn't know her well. I can tell you that she was a lovely lady and everyone liked her. Even me, and I didn't much care for anyone at the time."

Penelope felt tears coming.

"I'm putting too much pressure on you." Buzzardstock passed her a handkerchief. "I'm sorry I lost my temper. If you're going to do this, you've got to commit. Even in the face of difficult situations. If you want to succeed, you have to be willing to walk through fire. And you have to believe. If you can do that . . . the answer is in your hands."

"I feel like we're wasting time. Makara Nyx could be anywhere by now."

"Do you know the difference between a flat chisel and a V chisel?"

"Yes."

"Can you operate a die grinder without hurting yourself?"

"Yes."

"Then you're not wasting time. You're learning. Sweet Penelope! You don't need to know *why* right now. You just need to know *how*."

"But why do *you* do it? You gave up everything."

"Do I do it to chase my father's ghost? Perhaps. But I also do it because I look at a block of ice and I see things: Tattered flags! Rotting fruit! Jealous duchesses spying on scoundrel dukes! Love and hate and angles and noise—entire universes of possibilities. Most people just see a block of ice."

Penelope gestured toward her block of ice, which still looked like a giant humpbacked pickle with a tail. "What do you see here?"

"I see a chance for a strong girl to prove herself, if she works hard enough."

CHAPTER 20

Russell March leaned on the steel ice chopper, exhausted. He'd been working the field for so long that the cold sweat on his neck had dried and re-emerged at least a dozen times already. He squinted into his bucket, but he already knew what was in there.

Nine turnips. Nine lousy turnips.

That was all he had to show for eight hours of backbreaking work. Such was the life of a turnip icer. Despite the slow thaw of Glacier Cove, the town's ever-stubborn turnips managed to grow only under the thickest, roughest ice patches. "I know you little buggers are under there," he grunted.

"See, that right there is your problem, mate," said Hank Wimberley, his cheery work partner. "They can hear you."

"Oh, is that right?"

"Sure. You've got to flatter a turnip. Sing to it. Compliment it." Hank gestured to his own bucket, which overflowed with gorgeous leafy greens and swollen purple-white bulbs. "Treat it like a woman you love, and it will repay you every time."

"I can't wait to tell Marge you're treating her the same way you treat a turnip."

"Oh, Marge is far more bitter. Then again, she doesn't need to be scrubbed with a vegetable brush."

Both men grinned and went back to work. Russell began to think of how good a shower and a quiet evening at home would feel. Maybe a drink. He glanced in the bucket again. Still nine turnips.

"Oh, by the way," Hank said. "I hope Penelope is feeling better."

Russell stopped. "Penelope? What are you talking about?"

"My lovely daughter told me she wasn't at school again yesterday."

"Penelope went to school yesterday."

"Lilith said Penelope has missed a bunch of school. Just assumed she was sick."

Russell tried to smile, but he looked more like a man who had stubbed his toe. No, his entire foot. "Well, now, Hank, that's news to me."

"Oh." Hank grimaced. "I suppose I'm happy that she's well, but . . . Oh, Marge is right, I should just keep my big mouth shut. I'm sorry."

Unsure whether to be angry or worried or something else, Russell dug into the frozen ground again. But this time, he swung the chopper with such reckless fury that Hank, if he hadn't known better, would have assumed that his partner had some personal vendetta against the ice.

Coral sprawled on a blanket in the Cold Room, using Wolfknuckle as a pillow. She had grown bored with watching Penelope work and was reading the thick Nicola Torland book that Penelope had lent her.

Soon she got bored with that, too, and turned her attention to Penelope, who was lost in the *scrape-scrape-scrape* of the ice pick. "You getting along better with Ore9n?" she asked Penelope.

"We're good." Penelope enjoyed the company and was happy to make small talk. "He told me that

Wolfknuckle ate an entire shoe when he was a puppy. Laces and everything."

Coral shot a look at Wolfknuckle, who pretended to be asleep.

Penelope gestured to the book. "You like it?"

"Björg Baardsson is interesting. If the angry horde hadn't killed her auntie Elin and kidnapped Henrik, her whole life would have been different." Coral yawned and glanced at Penelope's block of ice. "Oh, it's a submarine," she said, as casually as someone might announce that today was Tuesday.

Penelope stopped.

When she took off her goggles, she saw Coral gaping at the rounded hunk of ice that had been her focus for the past three weeks. Penelope took a good look.

The long, tubelike body.

The hump on top.

The smooth, angular tail.

Now she saw it: The tube was the hull. The hump a conning tower and periscope. The tail? Rudder and propeller.

"Well done, my child," said Buzzardstock, who suddenly materialized.

Penelope rubbed her eyes. "How could I not have seen it?"

"Sometimes we're too close to see things as they really are. Other times, we're too stubborn. All told, a very reasonable facsimile. Here, take a look." He unrolled a scroll. "I sketched out a design beforehand."

Penelope compared the drawing to the sculpture in front of her. To her amazement, they were nearly identical. "You couldn't have shown me this sketch three weeks ago?"

"Now, where, my young pupil, is the fun in that?"

Coral gestured at a pair of small wings toward the rear of the sculpture. "What are these?"

"Hydroplanes," Buzzardstock said. "That's what makes the submarine move up and down. Otherwise, what use is a submarine?"

Penelope felt a prickle of excitement. But she knew by now not to ask questions.

"You've done great work here," said Buzzardstock. "I couldn't be prouder."

"He's right—it's pretty amazing," said Coral.

"Woof," Wolfknuckle agreed.

"Now," Buzzardstock said, "we go to work on the interior."

Without warning, Penelope threw her arms around Buzzardstock, who giggled like a child. Then she grabbed Wolfknuckle's rough paws and the two of them danced a short but jubilant jig. She even hugged Coral Wanamaker, which felt a lot like dancing with a telephone pole and about as rewarding.

"Because I don't appreciate being lied to, that's why!"

"But—"

"No." Penelope's father stopped stomping around the kitchen long enough to scowl at his daughter. "I don't want to hear it. The only thing you get to say is where you went when you should've been at school. That's it."

Penelope looked at Miles, sitting at the table right in the middle of the cross fire, picking at his turnip casserole.

"Dad," Penelope said. "It's no big deal—"

"Stop." Their father, who had never punished his children before, seemed flummoxed by the whole conversation. "So you're not going to tell me?"

"I can't."

"Fine. You're grounded."

"You can't ground me! I have to—"

"For the next week, you may not leave this house for any reason."

"You're punishing her for ditching school by

139

keeping her home from school?" Miles said. "Will you punish me too?"

Penelope stifled a laugh.

"You, shut it," Russell said. "Oh, she's going to school, all right. Both of you are. I'm going to walk you to school every morning. All week." He turned back to Penelope. "I'm your father, and I *demand* to know where you were."

"If I tell you, will I still be grounded?"

"You're getting grounded no matter what."

"Then why should I tell you?"

His face turned crimson with helpless rage as he stormed from the room in search of a pillow to punch. Though she knew she was in trouble, Penelope burst into laughter.

Miles didn't laugh. "I know where you were. Didn't I tell you to stay away from that weirdo?"

She patted her brother's hand. "Miles, you're my little brother. You don't get to tell me what to do."

"What were you doing there?"

Penelope explained how she had spent the past three weeks sculpting a submarine, of all things, and now they needed to hurry because Makara Nyx had escaped into the ocean and they were running out of time.

"A submarine?"

"I know. It's crazy."

Miles rubbed the purple bags that had taken up residence under his blue eyes. *A submarine? Why did that sound familiar?* He had never been on one, nor had he even seen one personally . . . and yet somehow the word rattled something deep in his brain. *Submarine.*

As he was squeezing the last toothpaste from a tube of Extra-Strength Turnip Brite later that night, it hit him. Miles *had* seen a submarine—in his own head. While standing over a bowl of melted candles at Wanamaker's Fortune-Telling Emporium.

He marched straight to the bedroom, where he found Penelope reading in her hammock. "Don't fall asleep," he said through a mouthful of toothpaste. "We're going to see your friend Ore9n with the silent nine."

CHAPTER 21

By the time the usual thud came from the kitchen that night, Penelope and Miles were ready. It was after midnight, and they'd been listening to the careless clinking of a glass against a bottle for hours. Miles disappeared into the kitchen and quickly returned. "In his usual position," he reported.

"Drunk?"

"Smashed."

"Drool?"

"Lots."

"Let's go."

Buzzardstock didn't answer the door when they arrived, so Penelope and Miles crawled in through the doggy door, dodging Wolfknuckle's enthusiastic tongue on the other side.

As they wandered through the soggy wasteland the house had become, Miles was shocked at how it had changed. The eyeball chandelier—gone. The vampire birthday party with the coffin cake—gone. A deranged trumpet screaming on an anthill clung to its shifting pedestal like a castaway on a lifeboat. Buzzardstock must have been partial to the bowling scene between the penguins and rhinoceroses, because he had pointed a high-powered fan at it to keep it intact. Both teams looked strangely appreciative of his efforts.

They found Buzzardstock lying on his back inside the submarine, chip, chip, chipping away at a panel on the wall. He'd been working nonstop and didn't notice his visitors until they were right beside him.

"Come in, come in," he said, like a kid who couldn't wait to show a new toy to anyone willing to look at it. "Right now I'm working on the engine room. See, here I've carved radio equipment out of the ice! Throttles, steering equipment, gauges, valves. The works. Oh! Let me show you the torpedo tube." The ceiling was so low that the three of them had to bend their knees and hunch their backs to fit in the passageway. "Here. Isn't that great? And over there are the ballast tanks. Follow me. Here's a series of semiprivate bunk beds, and beyond that the airlocked escape trunk. Look! I even made an ice cream machine!"

"This is incredible," Penelope said. "Have you slept?"

"I take a twenty-minute nap every four hours," Buzzardstock said, his eyes glazed. "I feel great! Let's have a cup of tea in the living room. Or shall I say the dying room."

When they got there, they understood what he meant. Most of his furniture was now puddles of water. The couch had shrunk into a love seat, so they found a dry spot on the floor where Buzzardstock laid out a blanket. "Well, now," he said, taking in Miles at last. "You certainly look . . . ragged."

Miles smiled thinly. "I can't sleep. I can't eat. I can't concentrate. And I saw that submarine a month ago—in my head. Your cookie did this to me, old man!"

"I'm sorry," said Buzzardstock. "Your sister told me you were struggling, but I didn't realize the extent of it. Yes, in some cases a dream cookie launches a chemical reaction in the brain that causes the neurons to fire improperly, altering the neural coding in your temporal cortex. It's like . . . well, the alphabet, but the letters are scrambled in the wrong order."

"What's in these stupid cookies?"

"Oh, you know, two and three-quarter cups of flour, one and a half cups of white sugar, a little baking soda, some nutmeg. I'll show you the recipe if you like—"

"I don't want the recipe. I want my life back!"

"Well," Buzzardstock murmured. "There is one thing. In rare cases, dream cookies essentially act as a poison. And there's only one antidote."

"Which is?"

"Another cookie."

"That makes no sense."

"Nor does a straitjacket full of spiders, my boy."

Five minutes later, a pair of plates sat on the blanket. In the center of each was a cookie.

Penelope eyed hers. Once Miles finally agreed that life could not continue as it had and agreed to a cookie, Penelope persuaded him he didn't want to go through this alone. She also understood that this was the next step in her journey. There would be no turning back from here.

They touched the cookies together like wineglasses and took a bite.

CHAPTER 22

Miles saw it first, and he didn't like it one bit.

One by one, every sculpture in the room came alive, staggering, slithering, decaying into a disfigured ugliness, wailing in regret. The sculpture of a partially melted grizzly bear stumbled from his barber's chair. No longer ice but rather an actual bear, he shook the water from his downy brown fur, roared, and looked around hungrily. A disoriented ostrich, looking more like a tree stump in a bow tie, began to croon an aria in a terrible squeaky moan. When a warped gumball machine opened up, sending hundreds of red, yellow, and blue spheres clattering to the floor, Miles felt strangely sick.

The scene appeared differently to Penelope. The

creatures drifting around did not seem menacing at all; in fact, they had a strange beauty. She wandered the room to get a closer look. Many of the figures stepped aside, whispering to each other about this curious girl.

One of the bowling penguins, a proud, regal specimen that Penelope had noticed many times, stepped forward. Dozens of medals shone on his perfectly pressed military uniform. He saluted Penelope with a stiff wing and looked her up and down with piercing black eyes. Mostly up. He couldn't have been more than three feet tall.

The penguin unleashed a series of high-pitched squeaks and tweets in a stern voice. He obviously meant to sound authoritative, and he would have, had he not been a penguin. Penelope stifled a giggle, which only seemed to anger the little guy. He launched another barrage of defiant squeaks.

"He says you're smaller than he thought you'd be," Buzzardstock said.

Penelope smiled at the absurdity of this. *Wait. How did Buzzardstock—*

"I speak his language," Buzzardstock said. "Or rather, I did a long time ago. But it's been a while. You'll have to bear with me. My Penglish is a bit rusty."

Buzzardstock sounded off with his own nasal

honks. The penguin nodded and responded sharply, and the two of them began volleying back and forth with increasing volume. Whether they were arguing, joking, or conspiring, Penelope felt horribly left out. "What's his name?"

"Beardbottom," Buzzardstock said.

"Beardbottom." Penelope smiled. "Will you tell him I'm Penelope March? And that's my brother Miles over there?"

The old man and the penguin exchanged more squeaks. "He knows who you are," Buzzardstock said. "Very serious penguin, this one."

"How does he know who I am?"

Beardbottom shuffled forward. He looked Penelope in the eye and began speaking in squeaky but otherwise perfect English. "Commanding Officer Philip Ulysses Beardbottom. Aquatic flightless armed forces, twenty-third regiment, fourth division. My crew." He gestured behind him at the gaggle of penguins, standing in formation, rigid and proud. "The finest naval birds in this hemisphere, or any other."

"Um . . . pleased to meet you. I'm Penelope March."

"We have been waiting for you, Miss March. Decker! Front and center."

Another penguin waddled forward, his posture straight as a metal rod, and chirped something in a staccato rhythm.

"In English, Decker."

"Sir, yes, sir!" he squeaked in an even higher-pitched tone. Then he turned to Penelope and saluted. "Executive Officer Frank Decker. Pleasure to meet you at last."

"Decker, please escort Miss and Mr. March to the craft and get them up to speed on our mission. On the double. We've got no time to lose." Beardbottom extended a flipper-like wing to Penelope, which was soft and oily when she shook it. His other wing, no more than a stub really, he kept pinned to his side. "I look forward to working with you," he said. "Rest assured that you are in the company of well-trained sailors of the highest order. Not a single member of this crew, myself included, will settle for anything less than success in this mission."

With that, he shuffled away, followed by two penguins.

Decker gestured to Penelope and Miles and cleared a path between the sludgy animals and objects skulking about on the Ice House floor. "I think you'll be satisfied with our operation," he said.

"Penguins make perfect sailors. We're smart, we're aerodynamic, we have binocular vision, and we don't sweat. And Commander Beardbottom is the finest flightless bird in the entire fleet. Superb tactical leader. A brilliant penguin."

Miles nudged Penelope. "Hey," he whispered.

"Yeah?"

"Are you hearing talking penguins?"

"Yeah."

"And they're in the navy?"

"I think so."

"Okay. Just making sure."

Decker looked daggers at Miles. "We also have very good hearing."

He pushed open the door to the Cold Room, and there was the submarine. But now, instead of the blue-white ice of which Penelope had memorized every inch, it was shiny and jet-black. And it was real. To Penelope's amazement—as if she could be amazed by anything else at this point—the ice floor was gone. The submarine was floating in water.

Atop the conning tower sat two uniformed penguins chatting. When they saw Decker, they jumped to their feet to salute him.

Decker frowned. He turned to the Marches and barked, "I present the AF *Delphia*."

Miles and Penelope had roughly a million questions stacked up like a skyscraper of blocks, but to take one out—any one—could bring the whole fragile thing crashing down. Safer to say nothing. Penelope spied a tiny opening on the side of the craft. Only when she saw another pair of penguins trundle out and down a gangway to a makeshift dock did she realize that it was a door. "How big is the staff?" she asked.

"The *Delphia* has one hundred sixty-five men. Though some of them are women. I would give you a tour, but I'm afraid the interior is a bit of a mess at the moment."

"Oh. Right. But I mean, how big are you? You know, as, uh, penguins."

Decker seemed offended by this line of questioning. "Yes. Well, we range in size from twenty-three inches—that'd be Twickie LaRouche—to thirty-eight inches—that's Ernst Popper, our independent duty corpsman. He's always been big for his age. But we don't differentiate between any two sailors. Each crewmember must be able to operate and repair every piece of equipment on board, no matter how large or small. And each has been trained to do the other's job in case of an emergency. Just as our missile technician knows how to make a krill omelet, our chef is fully capable of firing a long-range torpedo. Though I'm still not entirely clear on what *your* job will be during Operation Thunder Strike."

Miles cleared his throat. "Excuse me, uh ... Officer?"

"You may call me Decker."

"Decker. You said Operation Thunder Strike."

"Affirmative."

"What is that?"

Decker shook his head in a condescending way. "You really do know nothing. Operation Thunder Strike is the code name for our mission. In twenty-four hours, at oh-three hundred sharp, we submerge. At that point, our objective is fourfold: locate the subject, engage the subject, take possession of the subject's assets, and eliminate the subject by any means necessary. It will all be in a dossier, which our yeoman promised to have on my desk at twenty-one hundred hours. In *your* language."

"Is there some kind of problem?" Miles asked.

"No problem whatsoever," Decker snapped. "On

the contrary. I'm looking forward to holding the hands of two untrained children on board."

Miles and Penelope gave each other a look.

"Decker," Penelope said. "Who is this subject you're talking about here?"

"That would be Makara Nyx."

"The subject is a giant sea monster?"

"Affirmative. She's out there and we have some semireliable intelligence on her whereabouts. We'd urge you to keep all this under your hats. This mission is highly classified and extremely dangerous. Most likely, Nyx knows she is about to be hunted. She will no doubt respond with deadly force. But make no mistake about it," Decker brayed. "We will find the enemy, take her down, and recover the Shard. And you, for whatever reason, have been asked to come with us."

CHAPTER 23

"I won't let you." Miles pulled the clothes from Penelope's overnight bag. "It's as simple as that."

Penelope stuffed the clothes back in the bag. "Have you seen my flashlight?"

"Forget the flashlight—"

"Shhh. You'll wake up Dad." It was 4:45 in the morning. The sky was starting to go from black to gray. Penelope knew she didn't have much time before their father awakened, and each s from their mouths seemed to pierce the air loud enough to rouse him. Despite the fear that had seeped under her skin, she had promised Buzzardstock—and Decker—that she would return to the Ice House as soon as she had packed.

"What makes you think that submarine is even

safe?" Miles whispered. "The whole thing makes no sense. How can two kids, an old man, and a bunch of penguins fight a sea monster? If there even was such a thing as sea monsters!"

"Since when does the world make sense?" Penelope nosed around under her hammock. "I know I saw that flashlight somewhere."

Miles looked out the window. "What was that?"

"What?"

"I thought I heard something outside."

"I didn't hear anything. Oh! There it is." Penelope clicked on the flashlight, sending a beam directly into her brother's eyes.

"As your only brother on earth, I'm begging you, Penelope. Don't go."

"You'd rather stay and sink into the ocean with the rest of Glacier Cove?"

Miles switched tacks. "What about school?"

"If someone doesn't do something, there won't be any school to go to."

"Fine. I'll tell Dad."

"No, you won't," she shot back. "Even if you do, I'm going. You can't stop me, and neither can Dad. What's wrong with you? You saw what I saw! How can you not be packing your bags too?"

Miles began to say something, then stopped. In all honesty, the possibility of an adventure of this magnitude—and weirdness—energized him. Like everyone else on Glacier Cove, he had never left, nor had he been in the ocean, much less a mile underneath it. And all that fooling around with straitjackets and handcuffs? Those weren't escapes. Jetting off in a submarine filled with penguins: now, *that* was an escape.

"I want to go," he said. "But I'm afraid. We don't know what's out there."

Penelope patted her brother's hand. "I'm afraid, too, Miles. But I'm more afraid of what will happen if I don't go."

"You don't even know Penglish."

"I'll learn. We'll learn."

Miles crumpled to the floor and lay down.

"Can I ask you something?" Penelope said. "Did you see anything else in the future that you're not telling me?"

Miles tried to recall his nightmares and visions, but he was too tired. They had slipped away. "No," he said. "Just . . . don't leave now. They're not submerging for like twenty-two hours."

"Fine. I promise."

A moment later, Miles was asleep.

Penelope continued to pack in silence, stepping over her brother. After choosing some of her favorite books—and sifting through them in the dark, losing herself in adventures far away—she narrowed it down to nine. But as she was stuffing them into her bag, she thought of Decker. *"Pack lightly,"* he had said. *"Space is at a premium on a submarine. Take only what you need."*

Penelope didn't know whether she was leaving for a week, a year, or a lifetime. If only she hadn't lent *Nicola Torland* to Coral. Would she ever see these books again? As though betraying her dearest friends, she put them back on the shelf, zipped up the bag, and slid it into the closet. Then she placed the flashlight on top and climbed in her hammock to sleep for a couple hours before school.

Mrs. Shaw, the Marches' next-door neighbor, happened to be rising at that moment. She liked to get in her early-morning calisthenics before Mr. Shaw awakened. Halfway through her third set of lunges, she glanced absently out her window. She wasn't sure—because the dreary Glacier Cove dawn was known to play tricks on Mrs. Shaw's eyes, even before cataracts had clouded her world over—but she thought she saw, scampering away from the Marches' house, a small figure in black that looked like that strange Wanamaker girl.

Penelope and Miles didn't realize how tired they were until they felt the fog roll into their heads during the walk to school with their father.

"I'll be at work, so I can't be here to pick you up after school," Russell murmured as they reached the schoolhouse steps. "But this is a small town. If I hear from anyone that you two didn't walk straight home afterward, things are gonna get *real* interesting." He made a big show of not hugging them goodbye.

Miles groaned and walked inside. For some reason, Penelope stopped to watch her father walk away. Once he had crossed the street, he turned around, obviously hoping to catch a glimpse of his kids. When he saw Penelope looking back, he grimaced and gave her an embarrassed wave, as though he found this whole Being Mad thing ridiculous. Penelope waved back, feeling strangely sad.

Little of note happened at school, at least during the parts when Penelope had her eyes open. In history class, during a rip-roaring lesson on the biology of mold spores, her eyes grew so heavy that she had to prop them open with her fingers. Not even a barrage of spit wads in her hair, courtesy of more than one Funkhauser, could rouse her from her daze. Longest day ever.

When the final bell took pity on her at last, Penelope grabbed her things and sprinted for her locker.

"You going to the Shelf?" she overheard Ernest Kernwinkel ask Teddy Bronconato a few lockers over.

Teddy shrugged. "What's the point? The hills are all slush. That's not sledding. It's sitting in a bunch of puddles."

Penelope stopped. All she could think about was crawling into her hammock and drifting into delicious sleep so she would be on board and wide awake when the AF *Delphia* submerged at 3:00 a.m. But a new thought popped into her head. She decided to make a stop on her way home.

"Hello?" As the door slammed shut behind her, Penelope's voice faded into the thick silence of Wanamaker's Fortune-Telling Emporium.

The place was a mess—candles and papers scattered everywhere, dirty dishes stacked in the sink, a thick layer of dust coating the tapestries. From its sad little cage, the bird eyed Penelope as if to say, *Get me out of here. Please.*

"Coral? Are you here?" Penelope called out. Creeping through the wreckage, she felt better about her own little house. Then she felt a pang of sadness. How could a twelve-year-old exist in such a place? "I just came to get my book back."

A strange voice came from somewhere in back. Then again, louder. The purple bead curtains that led to the Wanamaker apartment waved ever so slightly. It wasn't a scream, exactly, nor was it ordinary conversation. It was a marble-mouthed growl, punctuated by odd shrieks. It might not have even been human.

Every instinct told Penelope to turn and run. But what if Coral was in danger? What kind of friend would walk away from that?

Penelope took a deep breath and crept toward the bead curtain. Through her coat, she could feel the hair on her arms standing up.

The bird chirped and flapped its wings furiously from its cage.

The voice grew louder.

When Penelope pushed through the beads, it

took her a moment to understand what she was look-ing at. Other than flickering candles, the room was dark. A figure dressed in a red hooded robe, its back turned to Penelope, huddled over some kind of altar. Strange shapes had been carved into a table. Thick wax drippings pointed to a silver cup in the center.

Between the shrieks and moans, the figure chanted in a low voice.

"Ri ni bocaj ello ulee, kee ba ri ni llaj en gou holo viz baraj vinye . . . Ri ni bocaj ello ulee, kee ba ri ni llaj en gou holo viz baraj vinye . . . Ri ni bocaj . . ."

As the figure reached for the cup with a wrinkled, splotchy hand, Penelope drew a sharp breath.

At the sound, the figure spun around, its hood falling to its shoulders.

It was Stella Wanamaker. But her lips had curled into a grotesque wave of chapped flesh, and her eyes had rolled back in their sockets to reveal only blood-shot slits.

Then she lunged at Penelope.

Penelope fell backward through the curtain, pull-ing the beads down with her until they skittered across the floor in all directions. She screamed and scrambled to her feet, banging her head against the birdcage and overturning a table.

Stella kept coming, eyes rolled back, arms stiff and outstretched like a blind sleepwalker. *"Ri ni bocaj ello ulee . . . Penelope March . . . Ri ni bocaj ello ulee . . ."*

Penelope turned and ran, screaming with each step until she was out the door.

By the time Stella reached the door, Penelope was halfway down Watermill Boulevard. In her wake, she left Wanamaker's Fortune-Telling Emporium with a demented old lady, a squawking bird, and an even worse mess than before.

Penelope probably should've run all the way home and locked the door behind her. But as she trudged over the crunchy landscape, the thoughts in her head bounced off each other so fast that she didn't know what to do.

How can I let Coral live with that maniac?

Should I tell my father?

Should I tell Buzzardstock?

How is it possible that Buzzardstock has created life from ice?

How can anyone find a shape-shifting sea monster in an enormous ocean?

How did penguins learn to speak English?

How do I fit into all this?

Will I even survive?

Beardbottom had made it clear that this mission could not succeed without her. But she kept thinking maybe Decker was right. What value could a twelve-year-old girl possibly offer on a submarine built for penguins traveling through an ocean into which she'd never ventured?

First she needed to find Coral and warn her about Stella. Where does a person go to disappear in Glacier Cove?

The Grotto.

The west side path looked completely different. Penelope's body ached with exhaustion and she wasn't sure she was even going the right way. The sun setting over the iceberg cast a weird pink glow over what remained of the terrain. "Come on, where are you?" Penelope said aloud. She knew the opening was around here somewhere.

As she leaped across a wide crevasse, Penelope's boots sank into the slush on the other side, and she felt the ground rumble beneath her.

A *pop* cracked the air like a cannon. Penelope, in search of more solid ground, shot back in the direction from which she'd just come. Across the crevasse, an ice mass the size of a football field broke loose from Glacier Cove and crashed into the ocean with a violent splash. Waves rippled away from what was once the coastline. Now it was nuggets of debris drifting into the distance.

One last fragment peeked above the water's surface for a moment, as if struggling to stay afloat. Then with one final gurgle, it gave up and disappeared under the water.

The Grotto was gone.

CHAPTER 24

Penelope dropped her backpack by the door and bolted into the kitchen, out of breath.

"Miles, you're not going to believe—"

She stopped before she was through the doorway. Sitting across the kitchen table from Miles, dressed in black and looking smaller than ever, was Coral Wanamaker.

Coral looked away, almost bored, as if it were the most normal thing in the world to be in Penelope's kitchen. Even more bizarre was what Penelope saw *behind* Coral.

Limping back and forth across the little room, trying his hardest to look stern, was Mr. Stingle-berry. Though all he could muster was an awkward frown, the kind of face one might make after taking a bite of something that has recently gone rotten, his presence alarmed Penelope.

At the other end of the kitchen stood Penelope's father, thick arms crossed, eyes burning with fury. "Sit down," he barked. "Now."

"I tried to stop them," Miles pleaded to Penelope. "They barged in—"

Russell held up his hand. "Stop talking." Then he turned to Penelope. "Start talking."

"Dad, I don't know what's going on here."

"What's going on? What's going on! What's going on . . . Well, now, let's see. You've been sneaking out of the house, disobeying my orders, lying to my face, and going to an old man's home to play with chain saws. That's what's going on. Then I ground you, make it clear that you're to walk straight home from school, and, for reasons I can't begin to understand, you go and do it again! Something like that. Is that accurate?"

"I can explain, Dad."

"I'll bet you can. All this nonsense about learning . . . what . . . ice sculpture? And floating off in a submarine in the dead of night with a bunch of penguins to search for a monster? Something like that? Is that your explanation?"

"That's ridiculous," Penelope said in a shaky voice. "Where did you get that idea?" She tried not to make eye contact with Miles, whose head was in his hands anyway.

"I was concerned," Coral interjected. "Worried that you were in danger. So I went to Mr. Stingleberry—"

Penelope sprang at Coral. "You little rat!"

Her father stepped between them and held Penelope at bay while she struggled to get loose.

"I went to Mr. Stingleberry," Coral continued, calm as could be, "and I told him about you and Buzzardstock. Our teacher had some alarming things to say about your friend."

Stingleberry ran his fingers through his thinning hair, as though he might find the correct words in there somewhere. "Yes, well, as you know, Ore9n Buzzardstock and I have a long—*hic!*—history. Not all of it's good. I . . . was a lonely child, and he took me under his—*hic!*—under his wing. But I began to see things. Things I could not explain. Just as he did with you, Penelope, he led me beneath his home and showed me a crystal. Said it belonged to a sea monster and that it was the only thing keeping Glacier Cove afloat or some sort of rubbish like that. And when I expressed disbelief, he turned against me."

"He's just a harmless old man," Penelope said.

"*Harmless?*" Stingleberry's expression changed. "Do you know why I limp, Miss March? Are you at all curious about that?"

Penelope said nothing. She was starting to feel ill.

"Your friend Ore9n Buzzardstock was teaching me how to smooth the edges of an ice sculpture with a pistol grip sander—I assume you know what that is—and he was displeased by my lack of progress. Do you know what he did? *Do you?*"

"I—"

"He cut off my toe with a chain saw!" Stingleberry bellowed. "Doctors couldn't even reattach it, because Ore9n Buzzardstock wouldn't give it back! Said I—*hic!*—didn't deserve it! My own toe! That's your harmless old man! He's a sociopath! A lunatic! A dangerous—"

"Okay, Paul, take it easy," said Russell. "We get it."

"Dad," Penelope said. "Listen to me—"

Her father put his hand up again. "I'm not going to lose my only daughter to this nonsense. Buzzardstock is obviously not right in the head. He's lucky there's not a mob on its way to his house to torch it to the ground."

The plausibility of such a scenario hung in the air for a moment, sending a tremble through Penelope. "Have any of you noticed," she said in a shaky voice, "that Glacier Cove is melting?"

Stingleberry snorted. "The size and shape of this town waxes and wanes constantly. It's—*hic!*—nothing new. That's the nature of an iceberg."

"No. That's not the nature of an iceberg. The nature of an iceberg is to float in ocean currents and melt when it reaches warm waters. When that happens, the iceberg can become unstable and tip up to a more stable position. That takes anywhere from a few months to a few years."

Stingleberry turned to Penelope's father. "This is the kind of claptrap he's filling her head with."

"Don't you wonder how Glacier Cove has survived so long?" Penelope asked.

"No," Stingleberry retorted. "It has survived. That's all we need to know."

"Oh, really? I just saw a hunk of the west side crumble into the ocean!" Penelope turned to Coral. "I also saw your crazy old—"

"Enough," Russell said. "Coral, you've been to

169

Buzzardstock's house. What do you think? Is he crazy? Is he dangerous?"

Coral tensed her shoulders until they were almost touching her ears. Then she exhaled and looked Penelope in the eye with a grief so overwhelming it seemed that her entire body might explode. "I wouldn't be surprised if he killed us all, then went home and made himself a sandwich."

Penelope's mouth plummeted. Her tongue stumbled to form a response. "She's lying!" She looked to her brother. "Miles, come on! That's not true and you know it!"

"I—I'm sorry, Pen," he sputtered. "I'm really sorry."

"Coward," she spat with such cruelty that the word seemed to strike Miles on the cheek, causing him to flinch. That was when Penelope felt the pressure well up in her chest—a mix of exhaustion and confusion—and boil over. She began to sob.

The anger in Russell's eyes softened. Within seconds, his arms were around his daughter, and her face was buried in his shoulder. As he ushered Penelope from the room, she was surprised to see Coral Wanamaker crying too. Russell dragged his daughter out and deposited her in her bedroom hammock.

After her father had left the bedroom and closed the door behind him, Penelope heard the click of a lock and bolt snapping into place outside her door. A few minutes later, she heard the same sound from outside her bedroom window. A prisoner in her own room, Penelope sank into the hammock and let the warm tears spill over.

CHAPTER 25

For hours, Penelope drifted in and out of delirious sleep. Whispers and raised voices, door slams and deathly silences crept in and out. The shadows under her door weaved their way into her troubled dreams.

She dreamed that Miles, Coral, Stingleberry, and Teddy Bronconato were playing Ping-Pong across from her hammock. While the ground rumbled beneath them, they argued over the score. Then Teddy hit an errant shot that struck Penelope's arm.

She woke with a sting and a start and found her father sitting on her floor, his back against the door, watching her. The clock said 12:35 a.m. The *Delphia* left in two and a half hours. She looked across the room at her brother's empty hammock. "Where's Miles?"

"Asleep in my room. Must have gotten tired of screaming at me. I know you both think I'm being a closed-minded fool. But I'm protecting you."

"Dad. You don't even know what you're protecting me from."

Russell rubbed his beard. "I know you and your brother are too smart for Glacier Cove and that you want more than anything to escape. But Buzzardstock knows it too, and he's using that to put some pretty dangerous thoughts in your head."

"And how do you escape? Purple Lightning?"

Her father cleared his throat and looked away. "I've only loved one woman in this world. I gave her my heart, and when she died she took it with her. A big part of me will always be missing. But the only thing that can come close to filling that hole is you and your brother. If I lost either of you . . . I couldn't . . . I can't . . ." His voice trailed off.

It was the first time Penelope had ever heard her father speak about her mother. She searched his eyes for signs of drunkenness. There were none. Penelope tried to hide the ache of sympathy she felt for him.

"A part of you is missing," she replied. "But half of me is a mystery to myself. I didn't lose Mom. I never had her to begin with. You've never once shared her memory with me."

Russell's eyes moistened. "I can't. I'm sorry."

For some reason the image of Coral Wanamaker's tears popped into Penelope's head. "What's going to happen to Buzzardstock?"

Russell's face hardened. "Forget Buzzardstock."

"But, Dad—"

"Just stop. Your brother begged me not to call the police, and I won't, but from this point forward, you won't be having any more contact with Ore9n Buzzardstock. And you certainly won't be getting on any submarine."

Penelope awoke to a faint clicking noise. Her father had fallen asleep, his enormous body sprawled out on the floor. He had his coat spread out over a tiny percentage of his torso and a hat wadded under his head for a pillow.

The clock read 2:42 a.m. Penelope had abandoned hope.

Then she heard it again.

Click.

Russell began to stir on the floor.

Penelope sat up. The sound was coming from just beyond her window. She tiptoed across the room, making sure the whole way that her father's eyes were closed.

Outside the window was Miles, backpack on, sticking a paper clip into the lock and twisting it to and fro. Struggling to boost him up to the window were two penguins in military uniforms. "A little higher, guys," Miles whispered.

Penelope had to bite her lip to keep from laughing. The penguins chirped at each other in obvious pain and inched her brother's body upward as he continued to work on the lock. Penelope could have kissed all three of them.

An emphatic grunt from behind Penelope punctured the room's silence. Russell was tossing and turning on the floor. One more sound, any sound, would surely awaken him. Penelope's heart beat faster. She motioned to Miles and put a finger to her mouth.

"Would you two knuckleheads shut up?" Miles whispered. He continued to work on the lock, his nimble fingers darting in and out with the paper clip.

Click.

This click sounded different, fuller and more

satisfying, and when Penelope saw Miles pumping his fist, she knew he had done it. He slid off the lock, opened the window, and extended his hand to his sister. Still wounded from the scene in the kitchen, he could not meet her eye. "Wanna go for a ride?"

Penelope opened the closet door just wide enough to grab her overnight bag. But she forgot about the flashlight she'd left resting on top, which crashed to the ground with a clattery thud. Batteries rolled in all directions. One came to rest against her father's weathered hand.

Penelope's heart stopped, as did her feet.

Russell roused and sputtered. Then he scratched his beard and rolled over to face the other way. A moment later, the committed honk of his snores echoed off the floor.

Penelope tiptoed across the room and slipped the bag through the window. Then she slid her body through the opening into Miles's arms, whereupon the two of them, accompanied by a pair of sweaty and talkative penguins, left Russell March alone in a heap on the bedroom floor.

CHAPTER 26

The clock over the Ice House door read 2:54 a.m., and Buzzardstock looked relieved to see them. "So glad you decided to come." He clapped Miles on the shoulder. "Your sister I wasn't worried about. Well. Anyway, come, come. We haven't a moment to spare!"

As the old man ushered them through the remains of his house, Penelope eyed him curiously. Had he told her everything? The conversation in her kitchen had rattled her faith. She wiggled her toes in her boots.

The Cold Room buzzed with activity. Dozens of uniformed penguins scurried about, some carrying tools or supplies, others holding clipboards and barking commands in Penglish. One fellow dragged enormous frozen bags filled with what appeared to be slabs of beef. Another was stacking little computer keyboards and carrying them through a small door on the side of the *Delphia*.

"Some members of the crew were beginning to suspect you'd had second thoughts." The three of them turned to find Decker, rigid as usual, on the makeshift dock beside them. "I assured them, much to their relief, that that was not the case. Private Anderson. Their bags."

A paunchy little guy stepped forward and took a look at Penelope's bag. Though she hadn't packed much, it was roughly the same size as he was.

"It's fine," Penelope said. "I can carry my own bag."

Anderson looked back at Decker, who shook his head. The poor private swallowed and took the bag from Penelope's hand, staggering under its weight. "I'll come back for the other one," he groused, and stumbled off.

"All hands on deck!" an impatient penguin called out. The crew scampered around to finish their tasks, then filtered up the gangway through a small hatch on the side of the submarine.

Decker nodded at Miles and Penelope. Miles started toward the gangway.

"I just have a couple of questions," Penelope said.

Decker checked his watch. "There'll be time for that once you're aboard. We're scheduled to submerge in less than five minutes, and I don't relish the thought of explaining to Commander Beardbottom that I was the reason for a delay."

"If this mission is as dangerous as you say, then I'm entitled to a few answers before I board."

Miles shot a scorching look at Penelope: *You talked me into this, and now you have cold feet? Get on the submarine.*

Decker crossed his wings. "Very well. How may I be of service?"

"Well, for one thing, a few days ago, as far as I know, you were made of ice. How do we know you're not going to turn back to ice once we get down there? And is this thing safe? How are we going to understand what's going on?"

Private Anderson returned, his feathers ruffled, his beak dropping when he saw the size of Miles's backpack. The poor guy let out a whimper and dragged the pack across the dock.

Decker had turned his back to Penelope and looked up at the high ceiling, deep in thought, or perhaps so angry that he decided to end the conversation. Finally, he spun around.

"I am a military man. I don't ask questions. If a ranking officer tells me to stand on my head and whistle, I stand on my head and whistle. That's what sailors do. They follow orders. But I get it. You're not a sailor. So I'm going to tell you: there are some things about this situation that I've been asked to take on faith, and I would ask that you do the same. Yes, submarine combat under ice is less than ideal. Ice keels jut down into the water, which can puncture and sink a submarine if we run into them at high speed. But we will not. This craft is perfectly safe, and we are skilled technicians. Regarding us being made of ice, I'm not sure what you're referring to. We are flesh and blood and always have been. And every crew member has been instructed to speak English, for *your* benefit, for the duration of the mission. You and your brother will not be left in the dark. Now, come aboard." Decker turned and disappeared into the submarine.

"All hands on deck!" a penguin called again.

Miles ducked inside before he could chicken out. Penelope was alone on the dock.

"Bon voyage."

Standing behind her, with a bittersweet look on his face, was Buzzardstock.

"Wait," Penelope said. "You're not coming?"

"My faithful companion and I will hold down the fort here, at least what's left of it, and hope that your mission is a rousing success. You can't have a ferocious dog running about on board anyway." Wolfknuckle wagged his tail against Buzzardstock's leg.

"But you got us into this! You said this was the only way to save Glacier Cove! Now you're backing out?"

Buzzardstock smiled wistfully. "My dear, I never was in. I'm an old man and far too inflexible to fold my tired body into a penguin submarine. I've done my part. The rest is up to you."

"But . . . we can't do this without you."

"Nonsense. You'll know what to do when the time comes." He motioned around the room, the last part of his home that was not melting. "Just don't wait too long. When you return, we can trade tales of glory. I've got a few of my own."

Penelope bit her lip. "Ore9n . . . did you cut off Mr. Stingleberry's toe with a chain saw?"

Buzzardstock raised his eyebrows, then leaned over and put his hands on his knees like a sprinter trying to catch his breath. At first Penelope thought he was hanging his head in shame. Then she thought he was throwing up. But then she saw that he was trying very, very hard not to laugh.

"Heavens! Is that the tale he's spinning? You want to know how Paul lost his toe? He saw a mouse—a very small one—and dropped the chain saw on his foot. And he didn't lose a toe; he lost the tip of his toe. Very lucky. Then the stubborn dunderhead refused to go to the hospital because he didn't want his parents to find out. As if they wouldn't notice their son's bloody foot."

A penguin poked his head from the submarine and tapped his little watch. "Let's go, let's go."

Buzzardstock handed Penelope a small box topped with ribbon and a red bow. "Don't open it until you've submerged." He offered his wrinkled hand for a handshake, and instead Penelope threw her arms around the old man. He seemed surprised at first, and then his brittle body relaxed. The harder Penelope squeezed, the more she fought back the nagging feeling that she would never see him again.

"Don't you worry, Penelope March," Buzzardstock

said. "Some people are destined for glory. Others are destined to drop a chain saw on their foot."

A whistle blew. Then a dive alarm so loud it rattled the Ice House's walls. Penelope ducked aboard the AF *Delphia* and a penguin closed the hatch behind her.

CHAPTER 27

Voices boomed from all over the submarine. While Penelope and Miles leaned against a ladder near the entrance to stay out of the way, each sailor around them knew exactly what to do.

"Sir, ship rigged for dive!"

"Sir, request permission to submerge ship to two-zero-zero feet."

"Request permission to attain one-third trim, sir."

"Very well. Take her down."

"Mark the dive point!"

"Dive, dive!"

"Open the main ballast tank vents!"

"Venting forward!"

"Venting aft!"

"We're at depth zero two zero . . . zero three zero . . . zero four zero . . ."

Down they went, slowly, or so it felt to Penelope. The submarine had no windows to give her any perspective. But she imagined the layer of ice receding above her like a white sheet lifted from a bed, the water growing blacker and thicker as they dove farther toward a barren and rocky sea bottom.

Penelope turned to Miles. "I'm sorry I called you a coward."

He shrugged. "I'm still scared."

"What made you change your mind?"

"I had a dream last night. It was you, leading an army into battle."

It sounded so absurd that Penelope almost laughed. But her ears hummed with a weird electricity. "What were you doing in this dream?"

Miles's face, grim and gray since all this started, came to life. "Following."

Once the sub was two hundred feet underwater and plodding ahead at four knots, a serious pint-sized penguin approached Penelope and Miles. "I'm LaRouche. But my friends call me—"

"Twickie, right?" Penelope said.

"How'd you know?"

"Decker told us."

The little guy's mouth fell open. "Decker talked about me? What did he say?"

"That you were twenty-three inches tall," Miles said.

The penguin looked mortified.

"He also said that you were a promising sailor," Penelope lied.

Twickie stood as tall as he could muster. "Twenty-three-and-a-quarter. Anyway, I've been granted the honor of giving you a tour. Shall we?"

"Ow!" Miles bonked his head on a pipe running along the ceiling. He was still getting accustomed to the constant lurch of the submarine, and glared up as though it were the pipe's fault.

"Do watch your head there," said Twickie. "The interior has been designed with"—he motioned to his compact body—"a smaller frame in mind."

"So I see," grumbled Miles. If he bent slightly, his head had two inches of clearance from the ceiling. He looked like a hunchback in a dwarf's cottage.

"You'll see that the craft has been equipped with all the latest military technology," said Twickie, leading the pair through decks and passageways, past the periscope, oxygen generator, auxiliary generator, and ballast tanks. The tight space rang with the hum and clank of machinery. "State-of-the-art digital visualization, infrared cameras, and three wide-aperture arrays that give us the ability to look up and down the sub's exterior."

"I can't believe how much stuff you crammed in here," Penelope said.

Twickie nodded. "Yes, ma'am. As Decker says, there's room for everything aboard a submarine except a mistake."

A round chap, eyes glittering under his sailor's cap, waddled up and stuck out his wing. Penelope shook it and looked down at his feet for some reason. He had on tiny rubber-soled tennis shoes, which looked pretty funny on penguin feet. She liked him immediately.

"This fine fellow is Douglas Floyd," said Twickie. "He's the yeoman in charge of all written correspondence on board and has prepared a dossier that will get you up to speed on our operations."

Floyd pumped Penelope's hand with a fleshy wing. "I'm honored to serve aboard this ship with you, Miss March." He narrowed his eyes at Miles. "You, not so much."

Miles's jaw clenched. "What? Why—"

Floyd fake-punched Miles in the gut. "Just kidding. You two are legends on this craft." Floyd handed Penelope a thick document. "Once you get your bearings, come find me. We'll talk about the mission over a glass of lemonade." And with that he scurried off.

Twickie led them to a floor-to-ceiling brown flannel curtain. He slid it open to reveal three levels of tiny bunks—each one a tightly made bed scarcely bigger than a baby's crib—connected by tiny ladders. "Here's where the crew sleeps. You two have the bottom racks."

Miles and Penelope exchanged a look. Each space would have been roomy and luxurious for a penguin, or a toddler. Miles and Penelope were neither. Their bags, resting beside the pristine bunks, looked cartoonishly large and disheveled.

"Wow," Miles said. "Small."

"By your standards," Twickie harrumphed. "By ours, more than enough room for privacy and a few personal belongings. Each equipped with a ventilation duct and a small reading light. Neither of you suffers from claustrophobia?"

"No."

"Good. Our staff undergoes psychological testing to ensure they're capable of living underwater in close quarters. Some can't handle it. Perhaps I could make other sleeping arrangements if these are not up to your standards."

"These are fine," Penelope said. "Thank you."

"Very well, I'll leave you two to settle in. You can put your bags in the lockers over there. We've got a long journey in front of us. Get some shut-eye, and when you awaken, we'll arrange a rendezvous with Yeoman Floyd regarding the mission." Twickie caught Penelope's eye. "Permission to speak freely?"

"I'm not in the navy," she said. "All I do is speak freely."

"If you don't mind my asking, what is this mission all about?"

"We don't know, exactly," said Penelope. "I was hoping you could tell me."

Twickie eyed the dossier in Penelope's hands hungrily. "I could . . . read the dossier for you and, I don't know, prepare a summary."

"Thanks for the offer," Penelope said. "I probably ought to read it myself."

"Very well," Twickie said, disappointed. "Read it carefully. Then you can tell me what it says. Ha-ha. Just kidding."

After Twickie had shuffled off, Miles and Penelope

stood over the bunks, making mental calculations: *If I put my elbows in that corner and my head over here, and hang my feet over the edge, maybe . . .*

"Which one do you want?" Penelope asked.

"Does it matter?"

Miles climbed into the berth on the right and tried to lay his head on the pillow, which was the size of an envelope. Penelope followed into her own bunk. She lifted the thin blanket and curled herself into a ball as best she could.

Exhausted, she closed her eyes.

Just as Penelope was drifting off to the rhythmic groan and sway of the submarine, an earsplitting alarm pierced the air.

OOOOOH-GAA! OOOOOH-GAA!

Sharp blasts of noise pounded every nook and cranny of the ship. Penguins groaned from the bunks. Others sprinted down the hallway. A high-pitched voice on the *Delphia*'s speaker system began squawking over the alarm, something about a code nine in the hold and how all crewmembers were instructed to stay put.

Miles poked his head into Penelope's bunk, hands over his ears. "What's going on?" he hollered.

Before she could answer, their bunk curtains swung open, and a barrel-chested penguin pushed Penelope's face into her pillow. "Penelope and Miles March," he barked. "Put your hands behind your head. You're under arrest."

CHAPTER 28

The crew watched the penguin shove Penelope and Miles against a wall and pat them down from head to toe. He had to stand on a chair to reach the children's shoulders.

Another penguin stepped in. "Hey, Popper. Take it easy. They're just kids."

Popper got in the much smaller penguin's face. "Watch yourself, Private, or you'll spend your next five watches scrubbing a sewer discharge pump with a toothbrush and a pair of skivvies." He turned to Penelope and Miles. "Come with me."

Together, they trundled down a corridor past scores of crewmembers and into a small room. Inside were nothing but a table and three chairs.

"What's going on?" Penelope asked.

"I have no idea," Miles said. "One minute I'm drooling on my little pillow, and the next a penguin is shoving me down the hall."

The door opened, and in stepped Commander Beardbottom, followed closely by Decker.

"Mr. and Miss March," Beardbottom said. "I apologize if you have been treated roughly. We take every precaution after a code nine. We will sort this out shortly."

Penelope stepped forward. "Sort what out?"

"Come with us, please."

Penelope and Miles followed them back through the corridor past the same concerned penguins.

Decker cleared his throat. "It seems we've had a stowaway in the cargo hold at least since we submerged. No one's quite certain how this breach of security happened, though steps have been taken to ensure it won't again. We thought you might be able to identify the intruder."

"Us?" Penelope asked. "Why us?"

Decker gestured to a small metallic hatch with a circular window at the end of the corridor.

Sometimes a person's brain hiccups when they see a familiar face in an unfamiliar place. That was the sensation that pummeled Penelope when she looked in the hatch window and saw Coral Wanamaker.

"What's she doing here?" Coral's pale and passive face rekindled Penelope's anger.

"I wish I understood it myself," said Decker. "Our security procedures are extremely tight, but somehow she snuck in and evaded scrutiny during the security check before we submerged. Now she refuses to speak. So you know her?"

"Her name is Coral Wanamaker. She lives in Glacier Cove, and she's in sixth grade, like me."

"What the devil is she doing on my ship?" Beardbottom boomed.

As Penelope watched Coral through the window, something unspoken passed between the two girls. "Forget it," she told Beardbottom. "Coral is a liar. And she won't talk."

"I wouldn't be so sure," Decker said darkly. "We have ways of getting prisoners to talk."

"Not this one. She's survived tortures far worse than yours."

"I sincerely doubt that."

"Have you ever been in sixth grade?"

Beardbottom stood on his tiptoes to peer in at this strange girl, who was silent and motionless, as though she were from another planet. "What does she know about the mission?"

"She knows about Makara Nyx," Penelope said. "And the Shard. Basically, everything Buzzardstock told me, he told her too."

Beardbottom turned to hide his fury. "Is she trustworthy?"

"She's the one who tried to keep me from getting aboard."

Beardbottom whirled around, his chest deflating. "Frankly, I'm surprised. The old man's usually a good judge of character. He obviously misjudged this one."

"Sir," Decker said. "We will not let her, or anyone else, jeopardize Operation Thunder Strike. Rest assured, she will be punished."

Beardbottom went toe-to-toe with Decker. "You will not torture this prisoner. Do you hear me?"

"Sir, yes, sir."

The commander took one last look at Coral and walked off.

"Throw her in solitary," Decker told his men. "If she won't talk, that's the only place for her."

Coral was handcuffed and led away by no fewer than fifteen penguins. It was a pretty ridiculous procession. Even with her tiny frame, Coral towered over her captors. She probably could have kicked them half across the ocean without trying. But she did not protest. Nor did she make eye contact with Penelope as she passed.

Decker turned to Penelope. "She's an odd one, that friend of yours."

"She's not my friend," Penelope shot back.

"Either way, I'm willing to bet she knows more than she's telling us."

"Of course she does. She's not telling us anything."

Decker seemed surprised by Penelope's sharp tone. "It appears the stereotype is correct—you humans *are* a prickly bunch. Perhaps you ought to go back to sleep."

CHAPTER 29

A rustling sound nudged Penelope's eyes open. She was startled to see, hanging upside down from the bunk above, three penguin faces watching her. Two of the three popped back up out of sight.

The third, a burly guy with mischievous eyes that twinkled with all manner of mayhem—even upside down—continued to study her.

"Hi," Penelope said. "Can I help you?"

"I've never seen a human up close. You're not as hairy as I imagined."

"Thanks?"

"I'm Omar. Special Warfare Operator, First Class. But I'm trying to advance to Chief Petty Officer."

"I'm Penelope. I'm trying to sleep."

"Well, wakey wakey, eggs and bakey, princess. You've been asleep for two days. And the officers are pretty eager to get you up to speed."

"Two days?" Penelope jumped up and hit her head on the top of her bunk, upending Omar temporarily.

"I wanted to wake you, but Martin and Lucas wouldn't let me," Omar said.

At that, the other two penguins popped their heads back down. "I'm Martin," blurted out a little guy with pointy elbows and thick tufts of black plumage above his eyes that resembled bushy eyebrows. "And this dapper gentleman"—he nudged the other one, a bony bag of an animal studying Penelope with soulful eyes—"is Lucas."

"Have you guys seen my brother?"

Omar plopped down on Penelope's bed in a silk sleeping robe. "Last I saw, he was in the crew's mess. But he might've moved on to the gym. We worked out together yesterday. Feel these paddle muscles. I can swim eighteen miles an hour. This breastbone here, it's like the keel of a ship. Okay, so I've got a little extra blubber around the middle, but that's how I withstand the harsh conditions. My body is built to fly. I just happen to do it underwater."

Martin squeezed onto Penelope's bed. "Pay Omar

no mind. That nearsighted barbarian's idea of high culture is wrestling and spiced rum."

"We're SEALs," Omar said. "I mean, not literally seals. I hate seals. Bunch of sneaky, oily blubber merchants. We're Navy SEALs. Sea, air, and land, trained in maritime military ops, and we were built for this mission. Check out this dense network of waterproof plumage."

Penelope glanced at the third penguin.

"Lucas doesn't talk much," Martin said. "Strong as a beast, though. Once stayed underwater for twenty-six minutes."

"Twenty-eight," Lucas said.

"The three of us grew up together, and we're ready to kick some tail!" Omar roared. The three of them slapped wings. "Okay, okay, enough with the touchy-feely talky. Now, who's going to ask?"

Martin smacked Omar on the head. Omar smacked him back twice as hard.

Penelope followed Omar's eyes to the foot of her bed, where they landed on the present from Buzzardstock. Someone had obviously opened the box and tried to rewrap it. And failed miserably. The paper had been taped haphazardly, the ribbon shredded as if by claws, and the red bow looked like someone had sat on it. The whole package was covered with black and white feathers.

Omar shrugged as if to say, *What did you expect? You can't leave a present unopened around penguins.*

"Don't worry," Martin said. "We didn't eat any."

Omar stared up at Penelope hopefully. "I really, really wanted to."

Penelope opened the package. Inside was a box filled with cookies and a note from Buzzardstock:

P: Use them wisely. I know you will. —Oregn.

The three penguins eyed Penelope as she closed the box. "Probably a good thing you didn't eat any," she said. "I don't think you guys are quite ready for these."

Penelope's stomach rumbled as she entered the mess hall. A rail-thin penguin wearing a puffy white hat popped his head out of the kitchen and thrust a spoon at her. "Taste this, yes?"

Penelope instinctively pulled back.

He pushed the spoon closer to Penelope's mouth. It was filled with clear, brownish liquid. "Hooked squid soup," he said. "It is delicious and nourishing, and the only one who does not agree is the one too stubborn to try it."

Penelope opened her mouth and the chef slid the spoon in.

"Well? You like it, no?"

Her face froze. "That is . . . amazing. I mean, like, the best thing I've ever tasted."

The chef nodded. "Culinary specialist Jean-Jacques Dupree. Your lunch choices today are spaghetti and meatballs with fresh-grated Parmesan, jumbo pepperoni pizza, squid soup, sloppy joes, potato chips, crispy double fried chicken, wagon wheel pancakes with fresh maple syrup and whipped cream, hot jelly-filled doughnuts, one hundred seventy-four flavors of ice cream, and a tower of chocolate cake. What would you like, mademoiselle?"

Penelope's belly had been deprived of non-turnip-related options for so long she didn't know where to begin. Around the mess hall, penguins chatted quietly, their plates and silverware sliding as the ship rocked ever so slightly. One table over, a penguin stuck a tiny fork into a mountain of something blackened and glistening. "What's that guy eating?"

"Sautéed krill. Delectable little fish. Can be prepared a thousand and one different ways, each of them *magnifique*."

"I'll have . . . the pizza, a sloppy joe, potato chips, two wagon wheel pancakes, a bowl of squid soup, and a scoop of ice cream."

"What flavor?"

"Chocolate?"

"Chocolate? Any flavor at your fingertips, any topping you desire? No, no, no, no, no. Use your imagination, *s'il vous plaît*."

Penelope thought for a moment. "I'd like a scoop of strawberry–peanut butter–fudge brownie ice cream topped with rainbow sprinkles and stuffed with chocolate chips. And caramel on top."

"And to drink?"

"Root beer."

The little chef disappeared into the kitchen.

Penelope ran her fingers over the leather-bound cover of Floyd's dossier, embossed with the following words:

MISSION: Operation Thunder Strike
CRAFT: AF *Delphia*
RT#: 101198796428

C/O: XO Decker; Cmdr. Beardbottom; P. March
PREPARED BY: Yeoman Douglas Floyd
SECURITY CLEARANCE: Highly classified
STATUS: Destroy after reading

She opened it and devoured every word. Words and phrases danced out at her—*long-range torpedo . . . targeted assassination . . . history of brutality . . . possibility of mass casualties.* She thought of Omar, Martin, and Lucas, so gung ho for action. Did they have any clue how dangerous this mission was? At various points, her mind drifted to Buzzardstock in his melting house on Glacier Cove and to Coral, who, according to Martin, had not spoken a word in solitary confinement.

Dupree brought out Penelope's lunch plate—actually four plates. She started slowly, savoring each delicious bite. Soon she was shoveling in everything, reaching for the sloppy joe, then the pizza, then the ice cream, then all three at the same time and no longer caring which was which so long as it wasn't turnips. She burned the roof of her mouth, got brain freeze, and dripped syrup down her chin. It was the best meal she had ever eaten.

Eventually she realized the penguins at the next

table were watching, mouths open in shock. One of the penguins mumbled something to the other two in Penglish. They glared at Penelope and nodded to each other. A minute later, they got up and left.

When Dupree cleared her plates, Penelope pointed at the empty table. "What did they say?"

"That humans eat like pigs. And that you have a chip on your shoulder."

"I beg your pardon?"

"No, literally. You've got a chip on your shoulder. Potato chip, I think."

CHAPTER 30

"Sit, sit," Floyd said. "Please, get comfortable—or as comfortable as possible, anyway."

Penelope looked at the little circular table in the yeoman's quarters. The four penguin-sized wood chairs looked like dollhouse furniture. She eased herself onto one, so low to the ground that her knees were practically over her head. But the chair held.

"I trust that you've explored the ship a bit?" Floyd asked. "Have you had a chance to try Chef Dupree's omelets? I'm told the krillburgers are also pretty good. I wouldn't know. I don't eat fish. How are your bunking accommodations?" He winked at Penelope. "Apparently you had no trouble sleeping."

Decker entered the room, stiff as ever. Floyd stood and saluted the officer.

"At ease, people." Decker tried to laugh, but it came out more like a nervous harrumph. He patted the dossier on the table between them. "I hope you've had time to digest this, Miss March, and you understand what we're up against. We must act quickly but deliberately. Would you care to summarize, Floyd?"

"Yes, sir. Various sea creatures that we've enlisted as spies and agents around the ocean have reported strange accounts in the past twenty-four hours. Giant shadows, horrible shrieks. Trails of mangled fish along the ocean floor. Of course, we're not certain this is the work of Nyx, but if it is, she appears to be moving west at fifteen hundred feet from the ocean's surface, roughly seven hundred fifty nautical miles from where we are right now. And she's killing everything in her path. Assuming a speed of thirty knots for this craft, it would take us forty hours before she was in torpedo range. She's got a big head start."

"So," Penelope said, "we're launching a torpedo at Makara Nyx?"

"Affirmative. We don't know for certain that she has the Shard, but without it on her body at all times, she'd be too weak to unleash the level of destruction we're seeing. We want to be careful not to destroy the Shard. . . ."

"But how—"

Decker smoothed his wing feathers. "That's where you and your brother come in. When we get within firing range, the two of you, armed with an elite amphibious troop led by our finest SEALs, embark on a special-ops mission to recover the Shard. Once you have succeeded and have removed yourselves from harm's way, we fire the torpedo."

"Then we collect you, pop a bottle of bubbly, and go home," Floyd added.

Penelope waited for more. "That's the plan?"

Decker and Floyd exchanged a concerned look.

"More or less," Floyd said. "There are certain details to be hammered out."

"How do Miles and I breathe underwater?"

"It will all be explained to you," Decker said. "Tomorrow, oh-four hundred hours. You and your brother will undergo accelerated amphibious training."

"I know this is a lot to take in, Penelope," said Floyd. "Why don't you go check out the library? I understand you enjoy books. We've got all the classics and plenty of rarities as well. Penguins tend to be pretty eclectic readers. And though we work hard, there is plenty of downtime on a submarine."

"But not for too long," Decker said before Penelope could get excited. "We expect you to brief Mr. March on the details of the mission. Within twenty-four hours, we will be on war patrol. At that point the ship must remain quiet at all times while we search for the enemy. When you're off watch, you'll be required to stay in your bunks. All off-duty hands will. The easiest way for us to get caught is by making noise, and I don't intend to get caught."

Miles paged through the dossier in the library, a glorious oak-paneled lair lined with books from floor to ceiling. "This is absolutely bananas! How are we supposed to . . . I mean, what if . . . Who's gonna . . . Oh, for crying out loud, it's just bananas."

"I agree. Bananas."

"Did someone say bananas?" Omar thrust his body into the library, followed closely by Martin and Lucas. "Hey, whatcha got there?"

Miles snapped the book shut. "Nothing."

"That your dossier? Operation Thunder Strike?"

"I thought this was classified," Miles said.

"Dude, we're SEALs. We know everything. It's our

mission too. The boys and I are itchin' to get some action." Omar's face darkened. "Even if it's against, you know, her."

A silence shrouded the library until Penelope said, "Why is everyone so afraid of Makara Nyx?"

The penguins looked at one another.

"You wanna handle this one, Marty?" Omar asked.

Martin inhaled sharply. "Years ago, a penguin, let's call him Roy, was off Snow Island. It's breeding season and Roy's doing his thing, you know, waiting for his egg to hatch, balancing it on his feet and covering it with his brood pouch and all that stuff. He's been there for two months, waiting for his wife to get back with food. He's huddled with the colony. They're all starving and freezing, wind blowing snow in their eyes.

"Just beyond the edge of the breeding ground, the water goes dark. Roy sees this . . . thing . . . pass by under them, like a shadow under the water. Before he knows it, a giant fin shoots out of the water. It's like a manta ray's fin but a hundred times larger. The fin swipes a row of penguins into the water. Takes 'em away. Like seventy or eighty, gone just like that. Guys standing a few feet away from Roy. The water turns

209

red. And the thing doesn't even stop. It keeps swimming and it's gone.

"Roy's terrified. His friends are gone, broken eggs everywhere. He spends the next five days with the survivors, still trying to incubate their eggs. When his egg hatches, Roy breaks down and cries. That egg turns out to be my mother. She was a few feet away from never being born. Which means I was too."

Martin shook his head. "We're talking about pure evil here. Nyx has no feelings, no reasoning, no nothing. She just kills. And she doesn't care. That's a bad combination. She could be anywhere, anything, anyone."

"Heck of a pep talk, Martin," Lucas murmured.

The five of them sat in the library and let Martin's words sink in. What could this tiny crew possibly do against an enemy like that?

Omar turned to Penelope. "So, wait, there aren't actually any bananas?"

At 0400 hours, after a breakfast of fresh raspberries and muffins, the March siblings were led into a hidden chamber behind the electricians' room. There they found Decker standing beside a transparent sphere with a hatch at the top. "This is an L-80 submersible vessel," he said. "A deep-diving pod ship capable of maneuvering and combing the ocean on stealth missions."

"That's so cool!" Miles exclaimed.

"Yes, it is quite impressive," said Decker, running his wing over the smooth rounded walls. "Made of titanium and steel. Equipped for independent voyages of up to six hours. Seats ten penguins comfortably. Or five penguins and two humans slightly less comfortably. You'll be seated in back. Climb in."

Miles and Penelope carefully lowered themselves into the ball and into their seats, which sank down low enough that they had a few inches of clearance from the rounded plexiglass ceiling. The dashboard had an imposing panel of knobs, switches, and dials.

"Don't worry," Decker assured them through the plexiglass. "Our team of SEALs will pilot the ship."

"So what do we do?"

Decker's beak curved into a strange shape, one that Penelope recognized as a look of disgust. "I understand that Mr. Buzzardstock has provided you with a full stock of . . . what do you civilians call them?"

"Dream cookies."

"Yes. These cookies apparently are crucial to our mission, and you'll be expected to bring them aboard.

From what our engineers tell me, if you ingest a few bites, both of you will be able to exit the craft at great depths without suffering any adverse effects."

"What adverse effects?"

"When you're fifteen hundred feet underwater, you can't just go from inside to outside. Normally if you try that, your lungs rupture, your brains boil, and it feels like a million bugs are crawling under your skin. Otherwise, it's pretty painless."

Penelope and Miles climbed from the sphere with stony faces, which seemed to please Decker. "But you won't have to worry about any of that," he said. "You have . . . the *dream cookies*."

At that moment, two muscular penguins strutted into the room. Each had a tattoo on their wing peeking out from under their uniform and a puffed-up cheek, as if they were storing nuts for winter. Both saluted Decker.

"At ease, sailors," Decker barked. "These are Chief Special Warfare Operators Sparks and Pooley. They will be copiloting this mission."

Pooley stuck out his wing to shake Penelope's hand, bone-crushingly hard. "Pleasure, ma'am."

Sparks stuck out her wing, too, and spat a giant wad of brownish-orange juice on the floor.

"For Pete's sake, get a cup, Sparks," Pooley hollered. "This ain't the tundra, sister. Here." He handed her his cup.

"Sorry." Sparks smiled at Penelope. "Krill tobacco. Tryin' to quit. Disgusting stuff, really."

Penelope liked her instantly.

Decker sighed. "I believe you know these gentlemen," he said, gesturing to Omar, Martin, and Lucas, who had entered the room slapping each other on the back. "You may have noticed that Commander Beardbottom gives this outfit an awful lot of latitude. Too much if you ask me."

"It's all latitude and no longitude," Omar blared.

Martin scoffed. "That doesn't even mean anything."

"It's a shame you clowns are such effective sailors," Decker said. "The only one who doesn't talk, talk, talk is Lucas over there."

Lucas grinned. "Saving it all up for your funeral, big guy."

Everyone hooted and high-winged Lucas and made a general racket until Decker reminded them that the *Delphia* was about to be on war patrol and a quiet atmosphere was necessary. Which made them laugh even harder.

But when Decker left, the SEALs were all business.

"Basically, we're cramming eight months of training into a few hours for you kids," Pooley said. "So listen good."

They learned how to keep out of sight while swimming, spot and defuse bombs, and attach a limpet mine to an object underwater. They studied rare photos of Shards from the past and got acquainted with the dry suits—puffy astronauty things that Pooley described as "a submarine you can wear." They learned how to operate the wireless voice system inside the helmets that would enable them to communicate underwater.

"Do we get guns?" Miles asked.

"You're children," Pooley said. "We're not giving you guns. Anyway, you won't need them. But you're crucial to this mission. Penguins can swim underwater for twenty-five minutes, tops, so if we're out there longer than that, you two are on your own."

Miles struggled with the onslaught of information. Penelope, on the other hand, picked it up quickly. It was basically spy training, and she was having such a blast that she almost looked forward to the mission inside the orb, which the SEALS called the Trouble Bubble.

During a break, while the others were playing

slaps with Miles, Sparks sidled up to Penelope. "How's it going, March?"

"Good, I think. I mean, I'm just sort of winging it here."

"Maybe so, but I've trained a lot of SEALs, and I'm impressed by how fast you're learning." Sparks wrapped her wing around Penelope's back. "I gotta tell you. I think it's super cool that you're the one."

"The one what?"

"The one. The missing piece that's going to help us get Nyx." Sparks grinned and spat tobacco into her cup. "When I heard it was you, I felt, you know, proud." She looked over at the others yukking it up. "Nothing wrong with the guys. They work hard and they're fine sailors. We girls, though? We've got to stick together. Right, March? Besides"—she held up her wing—"down here, we're all winging it."

CHAPTER 31

The seven of them—Penelope, Miles, Omar, Martin, Lucas, Pooley, and Sparks—departed at 0500.

In their enormous dry suits, Penelope and Miles felt considerably more cramped in the Trouble Bubble. As the vessel lowered from an airlock into the water, Penelope felt a trickle of sweat run down her temple. Miles couldn't hide his nausea. "Don't ralph in that helmet," Omar said. "Unless you want to live with it awhile."

Sparks and Pooley hit a few buttons on the control panel and the craft jetted off into the dark water, churning a frothy wake behind it.

Headlights shined a bright beam on the path before them, and Penelope couldn't believe how barren the ocean was—just a few sickly white fish, some depressed-looking krill, and a handful of disoriented squid. Otherwise, just blackness in all directions.

"Not much exists down here anymore," said Martin's voice in her earpiece. "Almost no sunlight reaches this far down to allow even the tiniest plankton to grow. The area is so cold and hostile, it's less a food chain than a prison populated by species that don't know any better."

"Thank you, Professor," said Omar.

"Sonar aboard the *Delphia* indicates an enemy at fifteen nautical miles west," Pooley said, rubbing his beak. "Why don't we just sneak up on her? Whaddaya say, guys?"

"Not too fast. Young Miles back there might lose his breakfast."

The craft accelerated and pitched downward into a giant mountain range more beautiful than any Penelope had ever seen in a book. They zipped between soaring ridges and deep valleys until they were near the scarred ocean floor.

That was when the crew went silent.

The picked-over corpses of every once-living thing lined the rocky ground.

Bush sponges ripped apart, sea urchins in shreds,

scallops and worms torn to pieces. Nothing had survived. This was not the work of nature. Something had come through here, bloodthirsty and indifferent, and annihilated it all. Penelope reached out to squeeze Miles's hand, which didn't feel like much considering they were both wearing thick gloves. But his shaking hand squeezed back.

Sparks tried to lighten the mood. "I'm curious. How do these cookies work, exactly?"

"I have no idea," Penelope said. "They just do. For us, anyway."

"What happens?"

"You feel like you're leaving your body and traveling through space or time, and seeing things happening. Other times, you're in your body, but it's doing things that bodies don't do."

"What do they taste like?"

"Eh. They're not very good."

"I'm showing something two-point-three nautical miles northwest," Pooley said. "Something dark on the ocean floor. Bank right, Sparks. Toward that tunnel."

Sparks turned the wheel and they sailed through a gravelly corridor that appeared to pulsate around them. The crew spotted the end of the tunnel in the distance of their craft's murky yellow lights.

"Everybody quiet," Sparks said. "Hit the lights. Interior and exterior." A moment later they were in a dark so pure that it seemed to go on forever. Eventually, the tiny black-blue glow at the end of the tunnel appeared, and they crept toward it.

The tunnel opened up to a deep and massive valley. Penelope felt the downward tug of the craft descending farther and a slight hum of pressure pushing against the vessel's walls.

The seven of them spied a dark object on the ocean floor.

"Prepare to deploy," whispered Pooley.

Omar, Martin, and Lucas unsnapped their seat belts and attached collapsible harpoons to their wings.

"You got those magic cookies handy, March?" Sparks whispered. "It's chow time."

Penelope reached into a paper bag and handed a cookie to Miles, then grabbed one for herself. Both of them gingerly removed their helmets.

As Lucas opened the airlock compartment under his seat, Omar and Martin watched the March siblings, wondering what exactly was going to happen when they took a bite.

"Hang on," Sparks said. "What *is* that?"

Everyone stopped.

Penelope pressed her face against the plexiglass to get a better look at the mass on the ocean floor but couldn't make out its shape in the dark.

"I'm going to turn on the lights," Sparks said.

"Negative," Pooley whispered. "It doesn't know we're here. Our best chance is to surprise the enemy. Turn the lights on and you take away our advantage."

"We can't go out there until we know what we're dealing with. For all we know, it's approaching us right now."

"Don't touch those lights."

"Mom, Dad, quit fighting," Omar said. "What's the plan here?"

Pooley and Sparks stared at each other for a minute. The two of them had an entire conversation without saying a word.

Pooley sighed. "Fine. Let's see what we've got. Light it up."

Sparks flipped a switch, and for a moment Penelope expected to see a monster outside her window, looking in. To her relief, nothing was there.

But the spotlight lit a path toward the shadowy object on the ocean floor.

"Whatever it is, it's not moving," Sparks said. "Let's go in for a closer look."

"What if it's a trap?" Penelope asked.

"Then it's working," Miles said. "Because we're going right into it."

They crept closer to the ocean floor until the lights were shining directly on the object.

It was an airplane, a four-seat twin-engine plane with a rusted body, once silver, now a dull gray. Moss and seaweed draped its propeller and tail. Painted on the side were some strange symbols, including a faded image of a white flag with a red dot in the center. Beneath the flag was one five-letter word.

"What's 'Japan'?" Omar asked.

No one answered. No one knew.

Sparks pulled up next to the plane and shined the headlights inside. Still buckled in their seats in the cockpit, with hungry sea spiders weaving in and out of their exposed rib cages, were two very old-looking human skeletons. That was when Pooley and Sparks agreed it was time to turn around.

CHAPTER 32

"Have you got any relative bearing grease?"

Penelope stood in the supply shack, feeling ridiculous. The supply chief, a gruff old broad wearing horn-rimmed glasses, gave her a sketchy look that seemed to go on forever.

Pooley had enlisted Penelope to help out with maintenance and sent her off in search of this stuff. "We're installing relative bearing and we need grease," Pooley had grumbled. "And hurry. This maintenance can't start till we get it."

After glancing at her assistant, the supply chief vanished into the supply shack. Penelope couldn't hide her aggravation. She had already been to the torpedo division, the operations compartment, Dupree's galley, and two bathrooms, and no one could seem to locate even an ounce of relative bearing grease. Still, she considered herself lucky. Miles had drawn janitorial ops and was currently down in the depths of the lower-level engine room degreasing the bilges.

They'd been on the *Delphia* for three days now, slogging west. Every now and then, the sub made a dramatic depth charge and the whole thing pointed so far aftward—"all angles and dangles," the crew called it—that dishes slipped off tables in the mess hall and supplies fell off shelves.

But the Trouble Bubble remained parked in its chamber behind the electrician room. Makara Nyx's trail had gone cold, and after the mysterious episode with the ghost plane, no one trusted the vague intelligence information anymore.

"This ocean is twenty million square miles, and Nyx is a shape-shifter," Penelope overheard one officer tell another. "It's like trying to find a particular blade of kelp."

"And we don't even know what the kelp looks like," the other added.

The monotony had gotten to the crew—the endless maintenance, the drudgery of work, the constant fire and flooding drills. It wasn't long before they were blowing off steam in the form of pie fights, poker games, and, when Decker wasn't around, sliding down the long hallways on their bellies.

Miles often seemed to be in the center of it all. Thanks to Dupree's food, and at least ten glasses of chocolate milk a day, he had put on some weight. He was even starting to act like a penguin. He'd begun eating krill. And on days when he wore a white shirt with long black sleeves, strutting around with his belly and long neck puffed out, he even looked the part.

Penelope had grown impatient and began to devour library books at an alarming rate. She'd even tried her hand at the books written in Penglish. Most of them, as far as she could tell, were murder mysteries, and in the end, the murderer was always a seal.

The supply chief returned. "Sorry, Miss March. We're all out of . . . relative bearing grease. You might try the auxiliary machinery room."

Penelope threw up her hands. "But they sent me to you!"

"Oh, uh, you know, I might've issued the last can to the boys in the engine room."

Once Penelope was gone, the assistant turned to the supply chief. "Relative bearing grease? Haven't heard that prank in ages."

"Eh," the supply chief said. "It'll keep the kid busy for a while."

Was Coral ever really my friend?

That was the thought scratching at Penelope as she roamed in search of the engine room. *Or was it all a scheme of some sort?* The girl had been so silent, and then so odd, then suddenly so friendly, then ruthless and immediately tearful, and now silent again, that Penelope didn't know what to believe.

And where is this stupid engine room?

After a wrong turn at the oxygen generator, Penelope ended up down a flight of stairs, lost in the deserted bowels of the ship. It was a steamy, stifling underworld with metallic walls and grinding machinery.

Down a long silver passageway, Penelope saw an abnormally tall penguin. She had begun to distinguish one crewmember from another and recognized this one as Ernst Popper, the dour and hostile corpsman who had been so rough during her arrest. In his wing he grasped a hammer. At his side was what appeared to be a hacksaw. He was studying a thick pipe that ran the length of the corridor.

"Hello," Penelope called. "Do you know where the engine room is?"

Startled, Popper locked eyes with Penelope. Something in his gaze stabbed her chest with anxiety. It was as though his whole face and body hardened, feathers and all, into something calloused and unreasonable. Then he shot her a curdled smile and swung the hammer into a pipe.

The clash of steel sent a tight pressurized spray of water shooting out. Then Popper pulled out the hacksaw.

"Stop!" Penelope screamed, but it was too late. Her tentative walk became a desperate sprint as she watched Popper dig the hacksaw into the pipe. The jet of water thickened.

Popper turned on his heels and scuttled into the shadows, forcing Penelope into a split-second decision. Rather than chase him, she put her hand over the gash in the metal to slow the water, which was now pooling up around her feet.

"Help!" she screamed. But her voice disappeared quickly into the noise. No one would be coming.

The pressure beneath her hand built mightily until she had no choice. She pulled her hand off the pipe and cold water shot in all directions. Then she ran up the stairs in search of someone, anyone, who could help.

CHAPTER 33

An hour later, Ernst Popper was dead and Penelope
was shaking in a tiny chair in the yeoman's quarters.

"It's a tragedy, of course," said Floyd, fighting back
tears. "But it's a good thing you stumbled upon him
when you did. Our technicians repaired the pipe before permanent damage was done. We're just lucky he
didn't cut into the hull. That would have been"—his
face darkened—"problematic."

"What was he doing down there?"

"I don't know. Ernst Popper was a fine sailor, a
strong and moral penguin. We've interviewed dozens of birds and none reported any strange behav-
ior from him. He'd been on countless missions and

never showed any signs of cracking. But it happens sometimes."

Penelope thought of the stony look in Popper's eyes. He had not looked crazy enough to sabotage the ship, then slit his own throat with a hacksaw; he'd looked controlled—even amused. A thought bubbled to the surface.

"What if it wasn't Popper?"

"Multiple crewmembers identified his body."

"No, I know. I mean, what if the one I saw in the passageway down there was someone else, pretending to be him?"

"Who would do that?"

"Makara Nyx."

Floyd narrowed his eyes. "If Nyx wanted to sink this submarine, I can think of easier ways than disguising herself as an independent duty corpsman. Why not just rip a hole in the side of the ship from the outside?"

"Maybe she's toying with us. Maybe she thinks it's fun to turn us against each other. Maybe she *wanted* me to find her. And maybe," Penelope said quietly, "she's still on board somewhere."

• • •

If Penelope's theory was right, Makara Nyx had succeeded. When the shock and sadness over Popper's death subsided and rumor got out that Nyx may have been disguising herself as a crewmember, penguin turned against penguin.

Tempers flared. Accusations mounted. Friends who had worked together for years began to suspect each other. A wingfight broke out between a sonar operator and an electrician, both of whom ended up with bloody beaks and a trip to the infirmary, where they continued to accuse each other. More than once, Penelope caught a penguin watching her closely, as if *she* were the sea monster. Or as if she had killed Ernst Popper.

While walking past the gym, Penelope saw Commander Beardbottom running on a tiny treadmill. Without breaking stride, he nodded at her in his regal way. "Miss March," he boomed. Apart from a few ruffled feathers, he appeared as crisp and ramrod straight as ever.

"Commander Beardbottom."

The old penguin looked around. "The officers have their own gym, but I like to work out here. Enlisted sailors are much more interesting."

She smiled. "Sir, I have a proposal."

"Proceed."

"I want to talk to Coral Wanamaker."

Beardbottom pushed a button to stop the treadmill. He grabbed a towel to wipe down his face and shook his feathers vigorously, as if to eliminate sweat, though his coat was waterproof. "What good do you imagine that would do?"

"None, probably. I just wonder if she might be able to help. And it's the nice thing to do."

Beardbottom put his wings behind his back. His tiny black eyes searched Penelope intensely. "If I've learned one thing, it's that ninety-nine percent of hunches turn out to be wrong. But if you don't take risks, you'll never find the other one percent."

"I'll be right outside," said Twickie LaRouche. "Just holler if you need help."

"Thanks, Twickie," said Penelope. She couldn't imagine what kind of help might be necessary inside Coral's cell, nor what kind of help little Twickie could provide.

Twickie puffed up his chest. "We need a code word in case you need help. How about . . . berserk? Wait. Cocoon. Cocoon? No, hold on. I've got it! Commando! Yeah, if you need help, just holler 'Commando.'"

"How about I just say help?"

"Oh," Twickie said, disappointed. "Yeah, that's fine too."

The tiny room, basically four concrete walls and a dusty bulb hanging from the ceiling, smelled like armpits. In one corner, hugging her knees to her chest, hands still cuffed, sat Coral. With hollow eyes, stringy hair, and hands caked with dried blood from all the nail-biting, the girl looked as if she was dying. Maybe she was. A tray sat beside her with a sad slice of white bread and a bowl of gray soup. *We give her one meal a day,"* Twickie had said. *"And she barely touches it."*

The lightbulb flickered off. For a moment, Penelope panicked at the darkness, but then it buzzed back on. She sat in the opposite corner from Coral, and the room was small enough that their feet almost touched.

She still hadn't forgiven Coral, but the sight of her wasting away filled her with so many emotions that she didn't know where to start. With questions? Accusations? Sympathy? Anger?

"I just wanted to say hey," Penelope blurted out. "I thought you might be lonely."

Coral gave no indication that she had even heard.

The two of them sat in a quiet so absolute that

Penelope could hear the girl's every shallow breath. She tried to read the thoughts in Coral's head, which was now down between her knees. Nothing.

The bulb flickered off and on periodically. Nothing else changed. The longer they sat, the less Penelope knew how to draw out the huddled lump across from her.

How did I ever think I could get her to talk? I can't even get myself to say anything.

After an hour of excruciating silence, Penelope had had enough. Her legs had gone numb and so had her brain. How did Coral manage to sit here, hour after hour? The girl's stubbornness impressed Penelope to no end.

Penelope stood on wobbly legs. "I just thought you should know," she murmured. "Your grandmother tried to kill me."

For the briefest moment, Coral's face flashed with an agonized frown. But it quickly disappeared behind her mask of defiance.

It wasn't until Penelope knocked on the door for Twickie to let her out that she heard Coral's weak rasp behind her.

"Don't go."

Stunned at the outburst that had split open the

silence—and how quickly it had faded back into nothing—Penelope turned around. She found Coral trying to smirk, though it seemed to pain her to do so.

"This is the best conversation I've had in days," Coral added. It took so much out of her that she closed her eyes in exhaustion. When her head dropped back between her knees, Penelope knew that was all she was going to get out of her.

As Penelope bunked down that night, she heard faint sniffles coming from the bunk above.

"You okay, Omar?"

"Just feeling kind of lonely," Omar said. "I miss my girlfriend."

"I miss my dad."

"Wanna see a picture?"

"Sure."

Omar hopped down with a worn photo of a penguin that looked exactly like every other penguin. "Her name is Teresa."

"She's beautiful," Penelope said.

"Thanks. She's a real pistol. And you know what? She loves me. I can't figure out why, but she does." He blew his beak in a hanky. "Hey, don't tell the other guys I was crying, okay?"

"Of course not."

"Does your father love you?"

"He does."

Omar winked. "Even if you're an evil sea monster?"

Penelope laughed. "Even if."

"Well, then, as much as you miss him, I bet he misses you more. Dads are like that."

Penelope thought of her father. What had he felt when he'd woken up on her bedroom floor and found his children gone?

"Hey," Omar said, back to his old booming voice. "I heard you struck out with the creepy girl in solitary."

"Boy. Word gets around fast."

"Yep. If there's one thing penguins like, it's gossip."

"Omar, I'm curious about something." Penelope didn't know how to word her question. "How did Buzzardstock make you real?"

"What are you talking about?"

"I mean, you guys were an ice sculpture in his gallery, and then you came to life. What was it like being frozen all that time? How long were you there?"

Omar gave Penelope a weird look. "I don't know what you mean. I was born off Hogan Ice Shelf, and I've been in the navy for seven years. Buzzardstock? He's just a guy who lets us dock the sub in his house."

"But . . . what about the bowling? The rhinoceroses?"

Omar bust a gut laughing. "I think someone's eaten too many cookies. Also, I think it's rhinoceri. Which reminds me." He pointed to the box in the corner of Penelope's bunk. "I tried one of your cookies last night."

"What? Why?"

"I don't know. Bored. Curious. Hungry."

"Omar! You shouldn't mess with those!"

"I know. Spent all night on the toilet. Never experienced anything like that before, nor do I wish to again."

Omar ambled off, his claws clicking against the floor, and Penelope's eyes shifted to the box in the corner. Before she realized she had even made a decision, her hands were reaching for the box.

CHAPTER 34

Now she was floating higher than ever, up where the sun wrapped her face in a golden glow and the clouds felt like a breeze stacked with pillows and cotton as she passed through them.

The warm glimmer faded, and Penelope found herself somewhere dark and dusty that smelled of melted wax. From the corner came the weak squawk of a caged bird.

Wanamaker's Fortune-Telling Emporium. She was back in Glacier Cove. There was Coral, looking slightly healthier but terrified as her grandmother pointed a long, sharp fingernail at her.

"It is time," Stella said in a horrible voice. "Time to fulfill our destiny. The shadow prophesy, foretold ages ago, is upon us. Oh, have I waited for this day!" She grabbed Coral's shaky hands. "The girl. She is the key to it all. She will lead us to the final piece. Only then will the waters boil black and only then can we join the Dark Wanderer in the forever. Do you understand what you must do?"

Coral nodded.

Penelope was floating again. Only now it felt less like flying and more like spiraling out of control. Images flashed by, barely long enough for her to process what she was seeing. But Coral appeared in each one:

Standing alone, arms crossed, on the sidelines of Lake Trenchfoot while everyone else aided in Miles's rescue . . .

Outside Penelope's bedroom window, ear against the glass . . .

Sitting in Buzzardstock's Freezy-Boy recliner, squeezing Wolfknuckle's neck roughly . . .

Leading a stump-tailed cat down a dark corridor of the Ice House . . .

Lurking alone in a rocky corner of the Grotto . . .

Sneaking aboard the AF Delphia *in the dark . . .*

And then the horrible images began hitting Penelope so fast and hard—Stella waving her hand through a flame, a chunk of Glacier Cove falling into the ocean, babies crying, teeth gnashing, knives flashing, dogs whimpering—that nausea began to overwhelm her.

The last thing she saw was a spider squeezing its body inside a submarine periscope and flitting up, up, up through the portal until it was outside, on top of the submarine and swelling into a giant manta ray with red eyes that did not dim even when it slid off the craft and into the darkness of the water.

Penelope closed her eyes and felt the world spinning. She didn't open them again until she was back in her bunk on the *Delphia*, soaked with sweat and certain that Makara Nyx had slipped away.

This time when she entered Coral's cell, Penelope kicked the tray of food. Mucky soup shot in every direction.

Coral jumped to her feet, prepared to fight. But with her hands shackled, her options were limited. When she tried to pounce on Penelope in hopes of biting her shoulder, she slipped in the soup and crashed to the floor instead.

Twickie burst in. "Everything okay?"

"Fine." Penelope never took her eyes off Coral.

The little guy eyed Coral on the ground, broth soaking into her black shirt. "Just so you know, you're cleaning this up."

After Twickie left, Coral opened her mouth as if to speak. Before she could, a tear fell down her face. Then another. Then she kicked the concrete wall and the tears kept coming, faster and faster, until she was heaving and sobbing, thick drops rolling off her chin into the salty puddle of soup at her feet. Eventually, she broke into a coughing fit, though there didn't seem to be much air in her hollow chest.

"Why did it have to be you?" Coral choked out.

"I don't understand," said Penelope.

"All I wanted was to see that stupid town at the bottom of the ocean," Coral rasped. "I was tired of being picked on. But then you were so . . . You're the first person who's ever been nice to me in my whole life. I really liked— Oh, I don't know anymore."

Penelope tried to link the threads Coral was dangling. "Your grandmother. I walked in on her. She was wearing a red robe and was about to drink from a cup. She was chanting these words: 'Reeny something—'"

"*Ri ni bocaj ello ulee, kee ba ri ni llaj en gou holo viz baraj vinye,*" Coral said quietly. "'She that lurks beneath the waters, give her your strength so that you may live in light.'"

Something inside Penelope's stomach dropped.

Her disciples are still out there, dozens of generations later, underwater and on land. They believe that one day the whole ocean will boil and everyone will die except the ones who pledge their devotion. And then they'll be re-united with their ancestors.

Coral tried to bury her head in her shirt. "I was supposed to stop you. Sabotage you. Make sure the Shard got in Nyx's hands and stayed there. Stella told me that was the only way I would see my parents again."

Penelope's fury faded. "Why did you sneak on board?"

"All the weapon fuel on this sub? One match would be enough to spread toxic gases into every compartment and melt the hull. Then the whole thing goes down. I was waiting for the right time. Then they caught me. And right here, locked in this stupid penguin jail, it hit me for the first time in my life: I'm not like Stella. I don't care about Makara Nyx. I don't think I ever did. This submarine was my escape. I was free! Free of school, free of my grandmother, free of Glacier Cove."

"You should have said something."

Coral wiped her eyes. "How could I possibly explain? I stood by and watched Miles almost drown on Lake Trenchfoot—and for what? Because I was scared of my grandmother?"

For a moment, Penelope wondered if the whole thing was an act: Coral's stumble in the soup, her parade of tears, the explanation, and now, playing on Penelope's sympathy. The girl was a master manipulator. Penelope was nowhere near forgiving Coral—let alone trusting her. "You've been lying to me all along," she said. "Why should I believe you now?"

"I'm sorry." Coral looked away. "I've done terrible things. Sometimes ideas get forced on you for so long you lose track of whether you believe them or not."

The lightbulb picked that moment to flicker off. The two of them sat in the dark, the only noise Coral's pitiful sniffles.

When Stella Wanamaker had warned Penelope not to trust a new stranger in her life, at first she assumed that meant Buzzardstock. Then she supposed it must be Coral. Now she realized the deceitful stranger Stella Wanamaker had seen in the candle wax was not Buzzardstock, nor was it Coral. It was Stella Wanamaker herself.

"Let's get you out of here," Penelope said.

A shuffle came from Coral's corner. Then, quietly: "How?"

The bulb went on over Penelope's head, once more flooding the room with light. Only now it looked somehow brighter. "Do you know where to find Makara Nyx?"

Coral's tired eyes came to life. They darted around the room, left, right, up, down, then everywhere at once and nowhere at all, until they landed on Penelope.

"Maybe."

CHAPTER 35

When word got around that the ship was headed toward a massive range of volcanoes in the northern region of the ocean—due to intelligence from Coral Wanamaker—the penguins went ballistic.

"First we rely on half-baked intelligence from a bunch of brain-dead crustaceans," Omar whined, "and now we're taking cues from a little girl who's proven herself to be a lying traitor? How do we know *she's* not Makara Nyx?"

The farther the *Delphia* ventured into the ocean, the testier the sailors became. Most of the crew was not sleeping much; it's not easy to fall asleep with one eye on the guy in the next bunk. Decker argued against Coral's release, citing her as a threat to the crew's safety until she could be proven otherwise. Beardbottom agreed but asked that she be given better food, which Chef Dupree delivered directly.

Twenty-four hours before their planned military strike—which still had no exact location—Penelope checked on Coral. The girl looked a lot better, not that she'd ever looked particularly healthy. But she'd gotten back some of her pale glow, and Twickie had taken pity and dropped off a few books, which Coral read on the floor. "They gave me a chair, but it was penguin-sized," said Coral, sprawled out on her belly. "I couldn't even fit one butt cheek on there."

"Coral," Penelope said. "Do you remember hearing any specific details about Makara Nyx's hideout? Other than the fact that it's in a volcano?"

"Nothing more than I've already told you."

"How did your grandmother communicate with Nyx?"

Coral swallowed hard. "She lit candles and went into a trance. Her eyes rolled back and her body started shaking. Then she babbled and shrieked these words and numbers and chants like something had taken over her body. It was hard to watch. You saw it once. I had to watch it every day of my life."

• • •

245

That night, Penelope couldn't sleep again.

"Miles," she whispered. "You awake over there?"

"Yeah."

"Me too," came Martin's voice from above.

"Same here," said Lucas.

"Omar? You awake?"

A ferocious snore blasted down from Omar's bunk. Penelope and Miles started laughing.

"Guy could sleep through anything," said Martin.

"Hey," Miles said. "What's the deal with Commander Beardbottom's wing?"

Martin climbed down to Miles's bunk. "Beardbottom came up during the First Avian War, and even then, he was brilliant. Former boxer, trained as a laser physicist. Toughest, smartest penguin in the whole outfit. One night, a sniper ambushed his troop on Wingfield Ice Shelf and blew off Beardbottom's wing. But Beardbottom managed to wipe out the rest of the enemy platoon with one wing. Seal bouillabaisse, all over Wingfield. PU Beardbottom went on to win every medal the Navy had to give out. The dude won't die. Do you know what the life expectancy of an emperor penguin is? Twenty years. Beardbottom is forty-one."

"I heard he's fifty," Lucas said.

"Forty, fifty, whatever. They're just numbers. He can still do more push-ups than any man on this vessel." Martin hoisted himself up. "I'm racking out. Got to be sharp tomorrow."

Penelope couldn't believe creatures like Beardbottom existed. Knowing the formidable old sailor was on her side helped—no matter how many wings he had or how old he was. They're just numbers.

They're just numbers . . .

Numbers.

Numbers!

Before anyone could ask what she was doing, Penelope had jumped out of bed and was sprinting down the corridor.

"The numbers!" she yelled as she busted into Coral's cell. "Do you remember the numbers?"

Coral lay on the ground in the dim light. "What numbers?"

"The numbers your grandmother used to chant during her trances. Can you remember them?"

"Sure. I heard it enough times." Coral twisted her face into an odd shape. "Six, two—and then she always paused—then two, two, six, nine, nine, six. Then one, six, two—pause—five, zero, nine, seven, six, six."

Penelope handed Coral a pen. "Write them on my hand."

62 226996

162 509766

"Okay," Coral said. "So what?"

"They're coordinates. Latitude and longitude." Penelope threw her arms around Coral. "We know exactly where to look for Makara Nyx."

CHAPTER 36

The crew packed every inch of the mess hall. The lucky ones got seats, but many more sat on the floor or stood on tables. Others hung from ladders or clung to stairways. More than a dozen hunched in the pass-through of Dupree's kitchen. In back, two penguins perched on Miles's shoulders.

Decker stood before the room with a giant map of a volcano. "Sailors, your attention, please!" he boomed. "As of this moment, it is essential that you put aside your suspicions and place your trust in one another. No more blaming. No accusing. We're a team. The only way we'll succeed is if we act like one. For a little background on our target, Chief Special Warfare Operator Sparks."

Sparks stood up. "A few years back, Pooley and I pulled a search and rescue up around Slippery Pike. My commanding officer called the area Lava Alley. Lots of enormous volcanoes, and they all look the same. It's pretty hairy in there. Took us two weeks to get the ash out of our feathers."

The audience laughed.

"On our way home, one of the volcanoes erupted as we were passing by. Lava spurting everywhere, bubbles oozing molten rock. In between these giant plumes of steam you could see electric sea snakes and some other rough characters mulling around. Closer to the sea floor were deep-sea vents spewing burning water. The old-timers called the volcano Brimstone Peak."

"Thank you, Officer Sparks." Decker tapped the map with his wing. "If our coordinates are right, Nyx's base of operations is inside Brimstone Peak. If currents and wind hold out, we will arrive within six hours. Once we're there, Operation Thunder Strike will go in two waves. Many of you will be among the troops that infiltrate Nyx's volcano from above—here—to divert attention from the SEAL team, led by Sparks and Pooley, which will infiltrate near the base—here.

It will not be easy. Brimstone Peak is a volatile rock. It could erupt at any moment. We have no way of knowing how heavily guarded it will be. For specifics, each section leader will brief his or her team. But first, Commander Beardbottom would like a word."

Beardbottom stared out over the crowd, as if to make eye contact with each and every member of the crew. Then he cleared his throat.

"In one hour, the AF *Delphia* is officially on war patrol. You know what this means. You know your roles. What you don't know is how you will respond in the moment of truth.

"Unlikely circumstances have led us to this moment. Some may call it luck. Anyone familiar with me knows I don't believe in luck. I believe in strength. The strength to listen, the strength to think, and the strength to act.

"Many of you have never seen battle. Those who have, you've never been in a battle this important. We are on the eve of a conflict to end the reign of terror that has devastated our world for generations. Our mothers and fathers didn't have the power to fight that oppression. You do. What are you going to do with it?

"We have allowed evil to thrive in our midst for too long. Why? Because we are evil? No. Because we are afraid. But there is nothing to fear. Stand up, do your job, and do it well in the face of difficult circumstances. If you fall in battle, consider yourself blessed, for you will have ended your days in a manner that few creatures, sea or earth, are granted—with dignity.

"Some of us will not come back. This volcano could be our grave. This ship could be our grave. But whether you perish tomorrow or as an old penguin looking back many years from now, this will be the moment by which you are measured.

"Did you show bravery? Creativity? Resilience? Did you follow when asked? Lead when needed? Did you believe in the penguin beside you and give that penguin reason to believe in you? Did you lend a wing if you saw someone struggling? If you struggled, were you brave enough to ask for help? Did you show compassion for your fellow penguin—whether male or female, young or old, regardless of shade, personality, or preference? Will you be proud to tell your story?

"I will be beside you in battle. If I can answer yes to those questions, I have no reason for fear. Death isn't half as terrifying to me as the prospect of living with shame.

"Good luck and Godspeed, sailors."

CHAPTER 37

Commander Beardbottom led 120 penguins in formation around the Trouble Bubble, their wings flapping in unison like ballet dancers in icy blue waters.

Inside the Bubble, Penelope whistled to relax herself. To call the feeling churning in her belly "butterflies" was too mild. There were butterflies, sure, but also bees and wasps and mosquitoes, maybe a few moths and dragonflies, too, all fluttering and fighting and stinging.

She felt slightly better watching the penguins glide effortlessly around her in a manner that did look more like flying than swimming. She'd grown accustomed to their awkward waddling, but now she understood. In the water, their bodies could not be more graceful. This was where they belonged.

"Penelope," Miles said. "The whistling. Driving me crazy."

"Driving everyone crazy," Martin said.

The scenery grew more rugged as the mountains and cliffs soared around them. The Bubble rose closer and closer to the surface, sunshine streaming into the waters from above. It was the first natural light any of them had seen in a week.

To his left, Miles spotted a creature lurking behind a rock. It almost seemed to smile, but when it did, two rows of razor-sharp teeth glinted in the light. "Hey," he said. "There's something by that rock over there."

"Commander Beardbottom!" Sparks barked into her headset. "Leopard seal at ten o'clock!"

Without a word, Beardbottom had the entire swimming fleet reversing direction. The seal, an enormous gray hunk of muscle, lunged at the penguin on the outermost edge, just missing its feet. In frustration, it slammed into the Trouble Bubble with all its weight. The force of a furious seven-hundred-pound predator rocked the vessel. The seal pressed its wet nose against the dome just inches from Miles before swimming off in search of another meal.

"How thick is this glass again?" Miles asked.

Pooley grinned. "That was almost seal versus SEAL."

"Thanks for the escort, guys!" Sparks barked into her headset. "Good luck."

Beardbottom's troops disappeared in the distance as they ascended ever closer to the surface, while the Trouble Bubble went in the opposite direction. Downward it plunged, back into darkness so pure that the headlights illuminated the sea only a few feet in front of them.

As they zoomed past thermal vents bubbling up from the ground, Penelope felt like she was diving into the center of the Earth. Though they had no eyes, colonies of swaying tube worms seemed to stare in disbelief as the strange vessel piloted by five penguins and two humans passed by.

They were close. Penelope could feel it.

Sparks turned around. "Okay, Marches. Do whatever you need to do with those cookies."

Penelope and Miles looked at each other.

Are we really doing this? Miles's eyes asked.

I guess we are, Penelope's eyes said.

They reached in their dry suits, into which they had each attached a waterproof bag filled with the rest of the cookies. "I'm going to eat two," Penelope said. "Just to be safe."

"Two?" said Miles. "I'm eating, like, nine."

As the siblings bit into their cookies, the SEAL team once again unbuckled themselves, strapped harpoons to their backs, and prepared to open the escape hatch.

Lucas, who Penelope had almost forgotten was aboard, stuck out his wing. Omar slapped his on top of it. Then Martin added his, followed by Sparks, Pooley, Miles, and finally Penelope.

"Whatever happens now," Lucas said, "you guys are my family."

A few minutes later, Penelope and Miles felt themselves carried by an unstoppable current through the water. The rest of the crew—minus Pooley, who stayed in the Bubble for communication purposes—was swimming in front of them. Each had on a headlamp, lighting the way just enough to see the piles of dead fish and mollusks lining the ocean floor.

"Hey," a voice boomed in Penelope's helmet. Though it sounded distorted, she recognized it as Pooley's. "You read me?"

"Loud and clear," Penelope said.

"Everybody else? Can you hear me?"

A chorus of *yeahs* and *sures* and *too louds* crackled into Penelope's earpiece.

"I guess I thought your crazy cookies would lead us right to the source, but, uh . . . well, I suppose we'll have to do this the old-fashioned way." Penelope heard Pooley spit into his cup. "Head twelve hundred meters south, then roughly four hundred forty meters toward the surface."

Penelope and Miles swam their fastest but struggled to keep up as they darted in between the jagged boulders.

Soon they were face to face with a fearsome rock. Flashes of fiery light from above lit up the volcano long enough for them to see everything: steam plumes, thick lava pouring down, vents bubbling with poisonous gas, giant sea spiders tiptoeing around.

"Any ideas?" Omar asked.

Miles watched in horror as a sea snake, long and striped, materialized from the darkness and slithered toward his sister. "Penelope! Look out!"

But it had wrapped itself around her leg.

"Get it off!" she shouted. "Get it off!"

"Just stay still," said Sparks. "Its fangs aren't long enough to get through your suit."

"You stay still! I've got a snake on me!" Penelope swatted at it with her glove.

"Take it easy. Let your body go limp."

Penelope closed her eyes as the snake coiled and uncoiled, its ropy body throbbing around her. Finally, it lost interest and swam off into the deep.

Pooley's voice buzzed in Penelope's helmet. "What's the holdup, bubbleheads?"

"Eh, Penelope stopped to play with a snake," Sparks said.

Nearly a mile above them, Beardbottom's troops had made their way to the peak of the volcano. They launched themselves out of the water onto the rocky surface jutting from the ocean. It was a brilliantly sunny day in the middle of nowhere.

Beardbottom put a wing to his beak for silence, and the penguins fanned out across the surface, in search of an enemy, an opening, a chamber—anything. All they found was more mountain.

Half the penguins launched themselves back

into the water to comb the sides of the volcano. Through the gurgling lava and clouds of steam, they scoured the giant rock's walls on all sides. Nothing.

Beardbottom was helping a group of privates overturn a large boulder at the northern end of the volcano's surface when a lieutenant lumbered up to him.

"Sir. There's no one here."

Did they have the wrong rock? Every sailor had assumed Brimstone Peak would be heavily guarded from top to bottom. But this . . . was it just another desolate volcano amid hundreds of desolate volcanoes? It didn't make any—

BOOM!

An explosion rocked the surface two hundred yards behind Beardbottom, sending penguins soaring into the ocean on impact and others sprawling for cover. An orange-black ball of fire rose to the sky. Beardbottom heard the screaming and he knew. Land mines.

"Send over a medic," he told the lieutenant. "Tell your troops to keep their eyes peeled. This whole mountain is booby-trapped."

Penelope's team heard the noise, but from underwater it sounded like the harmless pop of a firecracker. They swam upward along the mountain.

Pooley announced that they had reached the coordinates Coral reported and asked Penelope if she saw anything unusual.

"No," she said. "Not yet."

"Miles, how about you?"

"Just a bunch of penguins with little harpoons."

"You've been underwater for twenty-five minutes now," Pooley said. "Anyone who's not a human being needs to surface and catch their breath."

"Ah, we're fine," Omar said. "I could go another half hour."

"I could live down here," Lucas said.

"Negative," Pooley said. "I need you to surface. Can't risk it. We'll get you back down shortly."

Penelope and Miles looked at each other.

"We'll be back," Sparks said. "Keep us informed."

And with that, the penguins darted upward, leaving a stream of bubbles and two scared children in their wake. Penelope and Miles were alone at the bottom of the ocean.

Pooley knew they were scared. To keep things loose, he told them a joke about a petrel. But just as he got to the punch line, his voice stopped.

All Penelope and Miles could hear in their headsets was static. They communicated with hand signals as they probed the mountain, though there wasn't much to say. Both also felt an ominous flutter in their breathing and a dull headache. Was it possible that the cookies only worked for so long underwater and their breath would run out?

Penelope closed her eyes.

Come on, Buzzardstock, she thought. *Give me something.*

Immediately, the image of a giant fiery ball spreading over the clear blue sky filled her brain, an apocalyptic roar that drowned out screams fading in the wind. She saw a penguin's unconcerned black-gray feet treading on a rocky surface.

When Penelope opened her eyes, she saw Miles reaching for a flat metal object poking out from the mountain.

"Miles! Don't touch it!" she screamed. "It's a mine! No!"

He couldn't hear her, of course, and reached for the object.

Penelope darted forward as fast as she could.

Miles's gloved hand was inches away when she grabbed his leg and yanked him away from the mountain.

Miles frowned at Penelope: *What's your deal?*

Penelope pointed to the metal and mimicked an explosion.

They got a good look at the mine, a silver nubbin the size of a hockey puck. It was enough to blow them both to the bottom of the ocean forever.

Penelope tried to ignore the sudden pressure in her ribs and head. She noticed Miles's chest heaving faster, his breaths short and clipped, and now she knew: their oxygen was fading, and fast.

As Miles studied the mine, his elbow grazed the mountain ever so slightly, triggering a giant *snap!* and sending him flailing about in the water.

He was stuck in an iron booby trap that had been chained to the mountain. Its sharp teeth had ripped through his wet suit and torn a jagged slash in the skin near his shoulder. A thick stream of blood poured out as he struggled to get loose.

Penelope tried to help but couldn't budge him. The pressure had begun to sting the inside of her nose. She figured they had one minute, maybe two, until their breath ran out.

They were in deep trouble.

Miles's body began convulsing. Penelope assumed he was going into shock. Then it occurred to her: her brother was attempting to dislocate his shoulder.

But this was no straitjacket. The harder Miles flailed, the deeper the iron teeth clamped down on his skin. Then, all at once, a calm overtook him, and his mouth curved upward into a feeble smile. Through gritted teeth, he twisted his torso inward to the most gruesome angle.

With a sudden jerk and an audible crack, he did it. He was free.

Miles pulled himself from the trap, the hole in his shoulder raw and exposed. Once he was safely away from the mountain, he jammed the shoulder back into place.

Penelope couldn't watch, and by this point she didn't have time to. Nearly blinded with the pressure in her head, she felt her arms and legs going numb as she studied the mountain for something—anything—that could lead them inside.

When Miles saw the colony of flapping orange tube worms along the mountain, he felt a strong déjà vu. Something about the cluster, no larger than the entrance to the Grotto, felt familiar. Howling in silent pain, he used his one good arm to push aside the tube worms and peeked inside. With what little strength remained, he motioned to Penelope.

• • •

Pooley floored it. He'd never had any reason to go faster than 10 knots in the Trouble Bubble. But now he was doing 15, 20, 25, churning up water behind him and zooming in and out of the tight peaks and valleys with lightning-fast reflexes. No way he was going to let these kids die.

Two minutes later, he checked his coordinates: 62.226996°S, 162.509766°W. Yes, this was it. The spot that the Wanamaker girl had reported. But all he found was a bunch of tube worms waving in the surf.

CHAPTER 38

The inside of the volcano was deafening. A throb of hisses issued from all directions, one on top of the other. Below Penelope and Miles lurked a giant amber crater filled with lava, which charged the air with a thick orange glow. Struggling to regain her breath, Penelope peeled off her dry suit before it melted into her body. Beside her, Miles had managed to do the same. His shoulder did not look good.

Penelope tied her dry suit around Miles's shoulder to stop the bleeding. "You okay?" she hollered over the roar.

"Yeah," Miles said in a dry-throated rasp. "Little warm, maybe."

"At least we're breathing. And not burning up. Must be the cookies."

They stood over the pit and watched the lava crashing and pulsating like waves at high tide.

"What now?" Miles croaked.

"I don't know."

Penelope closed her eyes. A million memories whooshed into her brain. Then, as if someone had taken an eraser to a chalkboard, everything was gone. Blank. Silent. And she heard, very faint, Ore9n Buzzardstock's voice.

"If you want to succeed, you have to be willing to walk through fire. And you have to believe. If you can do that, the answer is in your hands."

A peace came over Penelope, and she knew, as clearly as she knew her own name. It was the only way.

"Miles," she said. "Stay here and watch for the others."

"Where are you going?"

She pulled her brother's frail body into hers. "I love you."

"Tell me what you're doing!"

"I'm going to walk through fire."

Miles looked down at the blistering cauldron of

lava. "You've got to be kidding! In ten seconds, you'll be nothing but a pile of ashes!"

She tried to pull away, but his one good arm wouldn't let go.

"Miles." Penelope smiled. "Do you trust me?"

"I trust you! I don't trust volcanoes!"

"This is one of those things I'm going to do no matter what you say or do. Now let go."

When Miles released her from his grip, he had a strange look on his face. "I'll go," he said. "I don't understand, but if it'll keep you alive, I'll go."

"No. It's got to be me. And we both know it." She put her hand on his cheek and scaled down the steep rocks toward the hissing pit. "Keep pressure on that shoulder. If I'm not back in one hour, get out of here. And tell them to blow this whole thing up."

Penelope's feet reached the edge of the cliff and she looked down. A stone rolled off into the abyss and incinerated immediately.

Believe.

"Hey, Pen."

She turned around.

Miles smiled. "I love you too."

And then Penelope jumped.

Her body did not burst into flames. In fact, when

Penelope sank into the lava, she didn't feel much of anything beyond a thick, stinging sensation, as though her insides had *become* lava. She might as well have been jumping through a cloud that had been painted orange by the sunset.

As she fell farther and farther, faster and faster, everything around her became a blur—not orange, not black, not anything but an intense whirl of colors. She felt her fingertips tingling.

When the colors stopped, Penelope found herself in a long white hallway. White walls, white floor, white ceiling dangling with white lights. It reminded her of a hospital, clean and silent and empty. At the end of the hallway was a white door.

At the sight of the door, Penelope's courage shriveled into nothing. A dread, pure and black, slammed into her with such force that it almost tore a hole in her. She couldn't move. Whatever lurked beyond that door, she knew she had to face it.

Penelope willed her rubbery legs forward. The only sound echoing in the empty corridor was her cautious footsteps.

With a trembling hand, she pushed the door open.

It was a large white room, as sparkling and sterile as the hallway. At first, Penelope thought it was empty. Then she saw a woman sitting in a white rocking chair in the corner.

Though her dark, wavy hair and sad brown eyes looked familiar, Penelope did not recognize her delicate face until the woman's look of alarm turned to realization, then dissolved into a crooked grin that made the wrinkles on her forehead dance mischievously. And Penelope knew.

It was her mother.

CHAPTER 39

"Penelope?" The woman jumped up from the rocking chair. "Is that you?"

The sound of her mother's voice poked at some forgotten corner of Penelope's memories. "Mama?"

"Shhh!" Penelope's mother whispered. "She can hear you."

Penelope looked around the empty room. "Who?"

"Her. She. *It!*"

"Do you mean—"

Her mother put a finger to her lips. "Come."

Penelope started across the room—

"Quietly!" her mother whispered.

Feeling silly, Penelope tiptoed the rest of the way. But when she sank into her mother's arms, every worry and fear and pain melted away until nothing was left but a little girl, safe and sobbing on her mother's shoulder. She wanted to stay there forever. "I've missed you so much," she murmured.

Her mother let out a strangled cry. "I've missed you more than you can possibly know."

Penelope didn't bother to wipe her eyes. The tears kept coming. "But I . . . I don't understand—"

"I know. I'll explain everything. First, let's get out of here." She clutched her daughter's hand. "I can't be in this room a minute longer, and she'll be back any second."

"Who?"

Penelope's mother looked over her shoulder, though nothing was there but a plain white wall. "*Nyx*," she whispered. Then she suddenly dropped Penelope's hand. "Wait."

"What's wrong?"

"You." Her mother backed away, a shadow of panic falling over her brown eyes. "You're not my— No, wait a minute— Oh, how can you be so cruel?" She crumpled to the ground. "Haven't you tormented me long enough? Just leave me alone, you horrible beast!"

Penelope stepped forward. "I'm Penelope Grace March. I'm twelve years old. I live at 1220 Broken Branch Lane in Glacier Cove. My father is Russell March, and my mother is Angela March. You. I'm your daughter. And I've been waiting my whole life to say that."

"Penelope." Her mother looked so sad and helpless. "Is it really you?"

"It's really me."

"She's kept me away from you and played with my mind for eleven years. I don't know who to trust anymore."

"Trust me." Penelope grabbed her mother's shaky hand and led her to the door. As she tried the doorknob, Penelope noticed the tingling in her fingers had crept down to her palms. Locked. From the outside. "Do you have the key?" she asked her mother.

"No."

The two of them tried to bust the door down. Once, twice, three times. The thick metal would not budge.

Out of breath, Penelope looked up at the ceiling, which was covered with white tiles. "Hey. Give me a boost."

Angela clasped her fingers together, Penelope stepped into her hands, and together they struggled until she had hoisted Penelope inches from the ceiling.

Penelope pushed a tile and it slid loose. "Just a little higher."

"I . . . I can't hold you much longer."

Penelope glanced down at her mother struggling to keep her aloft. The woman's arms and legs shook. She made one last push, and Penelope shimmied her way into the dark tunnel of an air duct.

Penelope looked down. "Give me your hand!"

Angela reached up. She tiptoed. She jumped. But her daughter's outstretched fingers remained out of reach.

A rumble emanated from somewhere nearby.

"I think she's coming!" Angela said.

"The chair," Penelope said. "Pull over the rocking chair and stand on it!"

As Angela was stepping onto the chair and thrusting her hand upward, Penelope's eyes settled on the necklace swinging back and forth around her mother's neck. It was an ornate silver chain dangling with a small crystal rod.

The Shard.

Penelope pulled her hand away.

"Darling," her mother said. "Give me your hand! She's coming."

Penelope's brain raced. "What's your son's name?"

"What?"

"What is your son's name?"

"Honey, we don't have time! Hurry!"

Penelope searched the eyes of the woman below for a sign. Any sign.

"Niles," the woman said. "Niles March."

Penelope felt like she'd been hit in the head with a cinder block. She could barely muster the strength to say the words.

"You're not my mother."

The woman glared at Penelope with hurt in her eyes. All at once the hurt transformed into a smile so revolting, so foul and acidic, that it was painful to look at.

Then the woman leapt into the air duct and everything went black.

CHAPTER 40

"Oh, what a shame!" Gloomy, low laughter echoed up and down the air duct. "This has been such fun. Miles, Niles. I was so close!"

Penelope couldn't see a thing. She couldn't tell how far the tunnel went in either direction, or if it went anywhere. She only knew that she was on her hands and knees, she was terrified, and that Makara Nyx was somewhere in there with her.

"You think," the low voice growled, "that you can waltz into my home, uninvited, and take what's mine?"

"The Shard isn't yours," Penelope said. "It belongs in Glacier Cove."

"The place with the turnips, right? Charming

town. It's true I had assistance from my followers. But when you consider the number of hours I
logged at that horrid man's house with the hideous
sculptures—not to mention that ridiculous penguin
submarine—I more than earned this piece of jewelry.
Once I dispatch you, your sad little island of misery
will sink into the ocean like so many others, and the
natural order of the sea shall resume."

Penelope flailed about in the darkness. "Where
are you? Or are you too afraid to show yourself?"

Nyx cackled. "The question isn't where am I? It's
what am I."

Penelope felt something with lots of little legs
scurry up her arm. She screamed and tried to swat
it away. Then she felt a stab of pain in her back. She
reached around and squeezed a thick and slippery
creature squirming up her neck. A foul odor filled
the air and Penelope felt rancid, sticky breath in her
ear, but when she tried to grab it—whatever it was—
she got only a fistful of air.

"Pen," came a weak voice from behind her.
"Help me."

Penelope spun around. At the other end of the
duct, bleeding and in obvious pain, was Miles. Relieved, Penelope crawled toward her brother as fast as

she could, only to watch his body morph into an army of rats, screeching and scrambling in all directions. Then the tunnel went dark again, and the screeching got louder until it was upon Penelope, thousands of rats biting and scratching, crawling over her, under her, up her pant leg, in her hair, everywhere. Penelope screamed and screamed until the rats scuttled down the hall and out of earshot.

"You can give me the Shard," Penelope snarled through her tears. "Or I can take it!"

"I must admit, I admire your spirit," Nyx hissed. "Join me. We have much in common. I, too, lost my mother at an early age."

"You didn't lose her! You killed her!"

"Silence! You know nothing!"

Penelope had found her opening. "You killed your mother and your father. Your own flesh and blood! Why? For power? For—"

Penelope felt a sharp slash on her chin and tasted the metallic tang of blood. The pain struck immediately, throbbing in waves along with Penelope's quickened pulse. The claw, she saw, belonged to a ghostly demon with a pale, repulsive face that disappeared into the darkness.

"I'm going to eviscerate your body and spit the

pieces into a lava pit," Nyx muttered. "I believe I'll start by plucking out your eyes. But . . . you've come all this way. I shall allow you to choose the form of your executioner. Anything you wish. Use your imagination."

Penelope's brain spun. The throb in her chin— and the tingle in her hands—made concentration impossible.

You have to believe. If you can do that, the answer is in your hands. . . .

"Out of time, I'm afraid," Nyx said. "I'll choose for you."

A tiny stream of light illuminated a spot far down the air duct. Penelope couldn't be certain what she saw, because it didn't look like anything she had ever seen before. All she could make out was a giant, scaly, throbbing slab of meat with rows of suckers and razor-sharp teeth dripping blood blacker than ink. Then the light flickered out again.

When the light came back on, the beast was a foot from Penelope's face. Two scabby limbs reached out for Penelope's eyes.

"Ice!" Penelope screamed. "I want to freeze to death!"

Nyx pondered this for a moment. "Yes, there

would be a poetry to that. Plucky girl from iceberg travels all the way to a sizzling volcano only to freeze to death? Wonderful irony. But allow me to improvise, if you will."

Penelope watched as the creature before her changed once more. The sound alone—a cracking, splintering rumble—was gruesome enough. Features hardened, limbs thickened, eyelashes and fingernails flaked off into blue dust. Within seconds, a solid ice version of Penelope's mother was facing her in the air duct.

It reached for Penelope's eyes.

Then a strange thing happened. At the exact moment the bony ice fingers began to pinch the skin surrounding Penelope's eyes, the girl reached for Nyx's neck.

Nyx unleashed a bloodcurdling scream, and Penelope watched as the creature's neck caught fire. The flame shot down Nyx's arms and ignited again near her wrists, sending a flash of fire around her icy body.

Penelope tugged the necklace from Nyx's black and bubbly neck. The Shard clattered to the ground.

She reached between the flames and screamed as the Shard seared her fingers. Somehow, she managed to stuff it in her pocket. It was still so hot that she thought it might burn a hole through the fabric.

By now, the blaze had lit the entire tunnel in a bluish orange glow. Black smoke filled the air. Penelope coughed as the heat reached her lungs, and she crawled as fast as she could through the corridor in search of an exit. She stayed just ahead of the dancing flames while the metal scorched her hands.

The duct was melting. Just before Penelope felt it about to collapse, she turned to see what Nyx had become.

In the midst of the violent inferno, she spied a small puddle of water.

Then the duct collapsed and Penelope crashed through the ceiling of the white room. She landed with a sickening thud next to the remains of the rocking chair.

The room was no longer white. Fire shot so high it caked the ceiling and rushed down the walls. Though she had to crawl between the flames, Penelope had no trouble getting out of the room: the door was gone.

As she sprinted through the corridor, the ceiling crashed down behind her. Beyond the far wall of the corridor—which was now no more than burning planks of wood—she saw that the volcano was erupting. Explosions of lava shot high into the air.

"Miles!" she called. "Where are you?"

Then Penelope saw her brother sitting on the ground in the last spot the blaze had not consumed, holding his shoulder. Next to him, laid out like folded laundry, were their two dry suits. And on top of each lay a cookie.

CHAPTER 41

Atop a table in the mess hall, Miles hoisted his chocolate milk. Everyone was there: Omar, Martin, Lucas, Pooley, and Sparks. Twickie and Coral Wanamaker, who had become friends. The technicians and engineers and machinists. Officers and enlisted penguins. Even Decker was there, almost laughing as Miles held court.

"Anyway, after Penelope and I got out of there," Miles said, "she basically had to drag me and swim as fast as she could—"

"In other words, painfully slow human speed," Pooley hooted, and everyone cracked up.

Miles grinned and adjusted the sling on his shoulder. "So we heard this rumble behind us that sent shock waves through the water and Penelope gave me a serious look, like *Don't look back.*"

"What exactly happened up on the surface?" one lieutenant asked, turning to Martin. "I heard you guys were all over it."

Martin blushed. "Well now, I don't like to brag."

"I do," said Omar. He proceeded to tell them how the SEAL team had surfaced, intending to catch their breath for a moment, and found dozens of penguins injured from stepping on land mines; how they'd managed to fight off a pack of hungry leopard seals that jumped out of the water in search of weak prey; how Lucas had harpooned the largest seal between the eyes; how Sparks carried two wounded privates on her back for a mile to get them out of harm's way; how Martin had radioed to Pooley for help, who radioed to the *Delphia*, who sent a rescue party to evacuate the troops before the volcano erupted; how everyone assumed Penelope and Miles had burned up in the eruption, along with Makara Nyx, the Shard, and the rest of Brimstone Peak.

"I found them wandering four miles from the strike zone," Pooley said. "And wouldn't you know it: Penelope March had the Shard! She was swimming with one hand and pulling her brother and somehow managed to keep the Shard from falling out of her pocket. Amazing. I still can't believe she did it."

"I can," said Sparks. "The girl is incredible."

"I underestimated her," Decker admitted.

Sparks lifted her cup. "To Penelope March."

"To Penelope March!"

Penelope lay in her bunk, curtain closed. The experience had drained her, mentally and physically, and she didn't much feel like talking about it. After surviving the ordeal, she had survived devastating leg hugs from Omar and a trip to the infirmary to get her chin and hand bandaged by the duty corpsman. Then she had gone to tell Coral—who was now bunking on the lower level—that everything was fine.

Somehow the metal that had sunk its teeth into Miles's shoulder had missed every tendon and nerve. They counted forty-two stitches in his shoulder, which would come out in a few days. He'd heal just fine. It appeared he would also have a crazy scar that one penguin noted was shaped an awful lot like a turnip.

So why couldn't Penelope enjoy the moment like everyone else? The images of her mother and Makara Nyx did not help, nor did the constant throb of pain.

Mostly, she just wanted to go home. But it would be three days until the *Delphia* reached Glacier Cove, and Penelope didn't know what she would find when she returned.

The party had spilled over into the navigation room, where sonar technicians were dancing a jig and warbling a sea shanty.

A lone sailor sat at his console, trying to ignore the merriment. "Cut it out, guys!" he hollered. "If you spill booze on the sonar, I'm not taking the blame."

"Come on, Higgins," one of the singers said. "Blow off some steam!"

Higgins put his headphones back on. Almost immediately, he picked up a sound on the sonar unlike any he had heard before. He pressed the headphones tighter to his ears. There it was again, from roughly two hundred miles to the west.

An eerie, high-pitched hiss.

It was not another warship, which he could have easily identified by the sound of its propellers. Nor did it sound like a merchant ship. He wasn't certain it was a ship at all. It could have been a whale, he supposed, but judging from the unusual tone and frequency, it would have to be an enormous one.

"Guys," he called. "You gotta hear this. I don't know what to make of it."

One of the other penguins put on the headphones and listened. A few moments later, he took them off. "I don't hear anything."

Higgins put the headphones back on. Nothing. As quickly as it had arrived, the strange hiss, whatever it was, had disappeared back into the ocean's shadows.

CHAPTER 42

That night, Penelope couldn't sleep. Again. She traced the lines of her envelope-sized pillow with her fingertips. The rough edges felt like sandpaper.

Every time she nodded off, Miles woke her by hopping down from his adjacent bunk to go to the penguin bathroom—all that chocolate milk—and groaning about his shoulder.

By the time her brother climbed back into his bunk for the fourth time, Penelope'd had enough. "Why don't you just go sleep in the bathroom?"

"I tried," he said. "But every time I rolled over, I accidentally flushed the toilet."

"Miles," Penelope said a minute later. "Have you ever wondered what happened to Mom?"

"Sure. Every day, for a while. Dad always told me to mind my own business, so I gave up. I always assumed it was . . . I don't know . . . All I know is Mom died and Dad survived."

"You blame him?"

"Why has he never said a word about her death? Or her life?"

"Well then," Penelope said. "I guess we have no way of knowing."

The mattress under Miles squeaked as he rearranged his body. "Maybe we do have a way." A hand poked into Penelope's bunk space. In it was a cookie. "Last one."

A lump clotted Penelope's throat and a shudder of unease rippled through her. "I don't know," she said. "Maybe some things are better left unknown."

"And some things aren't."

The last bite had just dissolved on Penelope's tongue when her sore eyelids began sailing into space. Soon they left her face completely. Then so did her eyes, her tongue, her ears, and the rest of her head. Not wishing to be left out, her body quickly followed.

Penelope landed in a homey little cottage. Flickering candles lent the room a warm glow, and smiling family photos lined the walls. The modest home almost seemed cheerful enough to withstand the punishing blizzard roiling outside. The storm's noise did not simply whistle; it roared in hatred. Windows rattled, the ground shook, and the flimsy walls of the house seemed to push in on themselves, the photos inhaling and exhaling with every gust of wind.

In one corner, a toddler sprawled on the floor, sucking her thumb and flipping through a book. In the opposite corner, a young couple huddled over a crib. The woman pulled a thermometer from the baby's mouth, triggering a high-pitched wail that rivaled the cacophony swirling outside.

"One hundred and five," said the woman over the noise. "We need a doctor."

The man looked out the window. Night had fallen. He couldn't see much in the blizzard, and what he could see didn't look good. Snowdrifts were already so high that he couldn't even spot the houses across the street. Snow continued to punish the landscape, not just from above, but from below and the side as well.

He pulled on his gloves. "Doc Engleterra is a mile and a half away. He'll be able to help."

The woman bit her lip. She didn't want her

husband to go out in this weather. But what choice did they have? Their boy—their beautiful boy.

The man leaned over the crib to kiss the delirious baby and caress his wet cheek. "My sweet Miles," he cooed. Then he kissed his daughter, who barely looked up from her book.

"I love you," his wife said. She kissed him and held him longer than either of them expected.

The man trudged into the snow and was immediately hit by a wall of white. He couldn't see. With every step he sank farther into a snowbank, while the storm kept coming harder and harder until it stung the parts of his face that his beard didn't protect. He was a strong man, but he might as well have been made out of paper.

In all honesty, he couldn't tell what direction he was going. But he pushed on as best he could, thinking of the little boy in the crib. He'd walk for hours—or crawl if he had to.

The man didn't see the avalanche coming. It hit him with the force of a train, lifting his body off the ground and hurling it through the air. Before he had a chance to scream, it had deposited him underneath a continent of white.

His mouth was full of snow, and he knew it was

bad. Any attempt to move sent a jolt up his spine. He started scooping snow, hopefully enough to create an air pocket, and tried to swim his way out. But while thrashing his arms and kicking his legs—groaning at the white-hot agony spreading over his back—it occurred to the man that he didn't know which way was up.

Feverish with pain, the man tunneled through the powdery snow. Through some miracle, he was able to drag his broken body to the top of a steep snowbank. When he poked his head through, he screamed in relief. He'd never been so happy to see a blizzard in his life.

Two hours later—frostbitten, delirious, spine shattered, gloves worn through, and hands crusted with blood—he crawled back in his front door and landed in a crumpled heap at the woman's feet. He had not made it more than fifteen feet from their door.

The woman cleaned him up and wrapped a sheet tight around his broken torso while balancing the baby on her hip. Then she placed the writhing baby in the crib and put on her coat, her hat, her scarf, and every pair of socks she had.

"What are you doing?" the man wheezed through his pain.

"I'm going out there."

"You're crazy! You have no idea how bad it is."

"Russell, if we don't get help, he'll die."

"You'll never make it! Are you insane?"

"No." She buckled her boot. "I'm a mother."

"Angela," he pleaded. "I love these children as much as you do, but I can't let you go out there! I'd rather die."

"Of course you would." She smiled a crooked smile and kissed her husband on the lips. "You're a good man."

By now he was crying as hard as the baby. *"Don't! Please!"*

"Penelope's asleep in her room. Milk's in the fridge. Remember to keep pressure on the back."

"Angela. No!"

The woman forced her way out into the blizzard and was gone.

CHAPTER 43

The *Delphia* surfaced in the Ice House on a Tuesday morning, but it might as well have been Saturday night for all Penelope knew. She ducked out the hatch and onto the dock.

Penelope hadn't gotten two steps before she heard Wolfknuckle barking. The dog pounced on her with such glee that he bowled over three penguins and nearly knocked Penelope back into the water. Which was the last place she wanted to go.

Once the lickfest ended, Ore9n Buzzardstock held out his arms and Penelope folded herself into them. They hugged for so long, a bottleneck of penguins formed behind them on the gangway. One of the penguins began hollering to hurry up already, but another guy smacked him and told him to shut his krill hole. Penelope and Buzzardstock stepped aside.

"How's my father?" she asked.

Buzzardstock sighed. "The search party gave up the hunt, but last I heard, Russell was still out there every afternoon looking for you. For a while, he had people convinced that I had killed you. Police were involved. Lawyers. It was not a pleasant week for anyone."

"I feel terrible."

"Terrible? No, no, no, my dear. But it's safe to say he'll be happy to have his children back."

"I have something for you." Penelope unzipped her bag—heavy with books that Floyd had let her keep—and pulled out the same box that Buzzardstock had given her before the voyage. It was stained and shredded and looked like someone had sat on it.

Buzzardstock opened the box. Inside, lying on a pillow of tissue paper, was the Shard. Next to it was a note written in Penelope's cursive that simply read *Thank you.*

Buzzardstock smiled and handed it back. "A splendid gesture. But it's up to you now."

"No. I'm not—"

"Yes, you are. I'm not going to live forever, you know."

The box suddenly felt heavy in Penelope's hands.

"Buzzardstock!" Miles pulled the old man into a bear hug. "We did it!"

"You did it, my boy. I mostly puttered about in my bathrobe and baked pie."

Penelope spotted Coral Wanamaker in the crowd, looking for someone to celebrate with. Their eyes met and Penelope gave her an enthusiastic wave. "See you at school," she called.

"I think we might be on summer vacation now," Coral mumbled.

"Oh. Yeah. Wow. I hope we don't have to repeat sixth grade."

"We only missed a few days. I couldn't take another year of Stingleberry's hiccups anyway."

Once a soaring, open space, the Ice House had melted into a colorless and claustrophobic one. No sculptures, no twisting stairways or balconies or slides. It was now more of an Ice Shack. Buzzardstock had made the most of what remained, carving it to reconfigure the house into its new, modest blueprint.

"Oh, Ore9n," Penelope said. "I'm so sorry."

"Don't be," he said. "I'm not. It's still a house made of ice. That's all I ever wanted."

As Penelope said her goodbyes in Buzzardstock's packed home, it felt like the last day of school. Most of the farewells were quick and pleasant (Pooley, Floyd), some more dramatic (Decker, who acted like they were best friends). She looked around for Omar, Martin, and Lucas, but they found her first. Martin was eye to eye with Penelope, which confused her at first, until she saw he was standing on Lucas's shoulders, who was standing on Omar's shoulders, who was struggling to hold them both up.

"Give it to 'er, quick," Omar grunted. "Before I drop you both."

Martin grinned and handed Penelope a smooth red stone. "I found this on the sea floor. Everything down there was gray and black, and here was this beautiful unexpected burst of color. Made me think of you."

Penelope flipped the stone over. All three had signed their names.

"Be good to that brother of yours." Martin kissed her cheek and the three of them tottered off.

"Miss March."

Penelope turned to find Commander Beardbottom's beak pointing up at her.

"In all my years in the service—a number higher than I care to mention—I have never seen the kind of courage you and your brother displayed. Not just in battle, but in adjusting to a new way of life. Whatever you went through, and whatever aftermath you may experience, know that you have my respect until the day I die." In one swift, crisp movement, Beardbottom put his good wing to his forehead and saluted Penelope. "Thank you, sailor," he said, and walked away.

Just when Penelope thought she had run out of penguins to say goodbye to, she spied Sparks sitting alone in the corner, a big wad of krill tobacco in her cheek.

"Hey," Penelope said. "Guess this is it."

"Guess so." Sparks stood up. "I'm not big on goodbyes, you know? But I gotta say, March, you're an amazing girl. You did us proud."

"I'll see you again, right?"

Sparks smiled and spat into her cup. "Definitely."

As Penelope and Miles walked the streets of Glacier Cove, the town felt smaller.

And it was. Some homes were gone; others were being rebuilt. Roads had cracked and buckled. South Shore Drive had disappeared completely. Everything felt more crammed and cozy, but the people, most of whom were on their way to work, looked happy. One man was so surprised to see Miles and Penelope he gave them each a turnip.

When they turned onto Broken Branch Lane, there was their house in all its ramshackle glory, looking exactly the same. It had survived.

Inside, Russell March was cleaning up from breakfast. He was about to leave for work, but he'd convinced Hank Wimberley to cover for him that afternoon so he could knock off early to search for the kids. *Maybe today's the day*, he thought.

When he glanced out the kitchen window and saw his children running full speed toward the house, his first thought was that he was hallucinating.

His second was that he would not be going to work that day.

He dropped the bowl in the sink and stumbled outside, where he met Penelope on the front lawn and threw his arms around her. Neither said a word. They hugged and hugged and cried and cried.

Russell pulled Miles into a muscular embrace;

then the two of them pulled Penelope back in and all three wept in joy and shock and relief and for about a million other reasons. No one wanted to let go. Russell had thought about this moment so many times—rehearsed it in his mind, even—but the monologue changed every day. Now that he had his children back, he was so emotional he couldn't remember how to feel. So he cried.

And just like that, they were a family again.

That night, as Penelope was putting the box that held the Shard on a high shelf in her bedroom closet, behind a dusty stack of books and puzzles she hadn't touched for years, her father wandered in.

"Where's your brother?"

"Taking a shower. He really needed one."

"Looks like you could use some new boots."

Penelope looked at her feet. She'd barely noticed, but her toes were poking from her shoes. "Dad," she said. "I'm sorry for the way I left."

Russell closed his eyes, and when he opened them again, he seemed relieved his daughter was still there. "You know, I've gone round and round in the past week. I was angry. I was scared. I was sad. I was worried. I was hopeful. I wanted to find you more than anything; then I was afraid of what I might find. But no matter how I felt, I never gave up. Never."

"I love you, Dad."

"I love you." He stroked his beard. "I won't ask about the bandage on your hand or that gash on your chin. Or Miles's shoulder. You don't have to tell me where you've been. Not yet. I just need to know that you're okay."

Penelope looked around her bedroom. The two hammocks, the desk, the little window. The sound of her brother yelping in the cold shower in the next room. She could still smell dinner, for which her father had tried something new and sautéed a turnip, then sliced it into crisp-looking discs with caramelized edges. No meal had ever tasted better to Penelope. Nothing had changed, but everything had.

"I'm okay," she said.

CHAPTER 44

For two weeks, a heavy snow pelted Glacier Cove. Temperatures dropped back to respectable iceberg levels, solidifying the ice once again. Kids bundled up. Snowplows rumbled. Dogs ran outside to pee, then scampered back into the relative warmth of their homes. The town had no idea how close it had come to annihilation.

Buzzardstock never spoke a word about what had transpired, and now that everything was back to normal, people seemed to have forgotten him once again.

Despite missing her final exams, Penelope March was permitted to advance to seventh grade in the fall. A pleading phone call from Mr. Stingleberry to the principal didn't hurt. He didn't want Penelope in his class again any more than she wanted him.

Over the summer, Penelope spent a lot of hours under thick blankets, reading in her hammock. She didn't go outside much. Her boots had worn through on the bottom, so she could feel the ice on her toes. In darker moments, she imagined various strangers to be Makara Nyx in disguise. Other times, she expected to find Stella Wanamaker waiting for her in the shadows with her eyes rolled back.

Penelope tried to explain the submarine to her father. Russell listened patiently, maybe amused, maybe alarmed. After a few minutes, though, he held up his hand. "You know what? That's enough. I'm happy that you trusted me enough to tell me, but . . . well, let's just leave it at that. My wallet's in the kitchen. Go buy a pair of boots, would you?"

Sometimes Penelope would think about something funny Omar had said or how good Dupree's pancakes were, but she had no one to tell.

As Miles's shoulder healed, she saw less and less of him. He lost interest in escapology and traded his handcuffs and straitjacket to a kid down the block for a bike. Most mornings, a gaggle of kids would come by and he would leave with them. No one cared where he had been; his smile was back and he seemed eager to get on with normal life. Normal didn't include submarines or magical cookies or Makara Nyx.

Every now and then, though, Miles dropped hints that he had not entirely moved on. One day Penelope found a note in her brother's handwriting stuck in her book:

What's black and white, black and white, black and white, and black and white?

She turned it over to find the answer:

A penguin rolling down a hill.

At dinner one night, Miles asked Penelope, out of nowhere, if she'd gone to see Coral.

"No," Penelope said. For reasons she didn't understand, she had not made any effort. Nor had Coral. "Why are you asking?"

"She seems like she'd be a good friend."

Penelope wrinkled her nose. "What makes you say that?"

"I don't know." Miles smiled. "Maybe I saw the future."

The trek to Edinburgh Discount Footwear was not a pleasant one. To avoid getting slush-bombed by a car speeding down Watermill Boulevard, Penelope dove into a ditch. For her trouble, she got a faceful of snowdrift.

Next to the shoe store, a For Rent sign hung in Wanamaker's Fortune-Telling Emporium window. With a twinge of fear bubbling in her gut, Penelope pressed her face against the cold glass. The space inside was dusty and empty.

"Penelope March? Is that you?"

Penelope spun around. There, under six layers and lugging a bag of groceries, was Teddy Bronconato. "Hey! I thought it was you."

"Hi, Teddy!"

"I heard you were back," said her classmate. "Man, we thought you were gone, gone." Teddy whistled. "We had a candlelight vigil and everything."

"Really?"

"Yeah. The class really missed you. They even missed Coral. I know a lot of kids weren't so nice last year, but when I heard you were okay . . . well, welcome back."

Penelope smiled. It was the longest exchange they'd ever had, and she had no idea what to say.

He smiled back. "I'll see you in seventh grade."

"See you in seventh."

Twenty-five minutes later, Penelope's numb toes thanked her for the new pair of insulated high-topped boots made with waterproof suede. To break them in, she began to walk, with no real destination. But as her feet thawed, they knew exactly where they would end up.

Somehow, it was Wolfknuckle who opened the door when Penelope knocked. The dog yowled enthusiastically. When she stroked his fur, he ran in excited circles until he was so dizzy he crashed into a wall.

"Anybody else home?" Penelope walked into the foyer. "Hello?"

She tried the kitchen: nothing. Living room: no one. In and out of rooms, she found only dead silence.

Penelope wandered into the gallery that was once home to the Ice House's most ambitious sculptures—but as of her last visit, home to nothing at all—and stopped in her tracks. In the far corner stood the entire crew of the AF *Delphia*. Her heart boomed. "Hey, guys!" she called out.

No one moved. Every single penguin stood motionless.

Puzzled, she edged closer. They appeared to be posing for a photo, but she didn't see anyone with a camera. Some had wings around each other or were caught in a laugh; others were grinning or saluting, doing their best to look tough in their crisp uniforms—a proud, tight team of brothers and sisters. Omar had one powerful wing on Martin's shoulder and the other on Lucas's. His twinkly-eyed grin looked so genuine that Penelope put her hand on his belly.

But Omar did not laugh, and he did not move. He was ice. They all were.

Penelope finally found Buzzardstock in the Cold Room. "Penelope March!" he crowed, and jogged over to greet her. The submarine was gone, as was the water. The room had gone back to the same cavernous workspace where Penelope had spent so much time.

There in the middle of the room, chiseling the corner of an enormous ice slab, was Coral Wanamaker. She looked totally different: Happy, well fed. Healthy, even.

Coral's face lit up. "Penelope!"

"What are you doing— Why . . . ?"

"The day we got back to Glacier Cove, I went straight to my room and packed a suitcase." Coral swallowed and made a face. "Stella tried to stop me, of course. She put every curse on me she could think of. Said that if I left, I would never set foot in her home again. I told her that was the whole idea. That I didn't believe what she believed. And that if she tried to hurt you, I would *end* her. Then I walked over here."

Penelope was flattered. And impressed. She didn't know Coral had it in her.

"Coral is staying on indefinitely," Buzzardstock said. "The girl is quite a rousing houseguest. All she has to do in return is learn the art."

"Ore9n calls me the Ice Princess," Coral said. "I kept asking when I could go see you. He said you needed time."

"I guess I did."

"We began to worry that you had returned to the sea," said Buzzardstock. "Or that maybe your father forbade you to leave the house again."

"No, I've just been taking it easy. I'm—"

"No need to explain." Buzzardstock cracked his old knuckles. "You know, Penelope, you're welcome back at any time to continue your education. You're far from finished."

"Thanks. I will." Penelope motioned to the ice. "So, Coral, what are you working on?"

"I don't know." Coral looked at the ice and smiled. "But I can't wait to find out."

That night, Penelope lay in her hammock, trying to finish a book. She always concentrated better when Miles was there, but he had zonked out on the living room couch. Her busy mind kept wandering. She decided she would go to the Ice House tomorrow. Just to help out.

She was about to turn out the light when she heard a knock on her bedroom door.

"I wanted to say good night," said her father from the doorway.

"Come on in," she said.

As he kissed Penelope on the head, she saw the small wooden crate in his hands. He thrust it at her in his awkward gruff way.

Penelope threw her legs over the side of the hammock and slid the lid off the crate.

Inside she found wedding pictures and love letters, earrings and necklaces. There were ticket stubs and birthday cards and papers and some sketches. And photos. So many photos. Penelope found a document from the mayor of Glacier Cove declaring May 9 to be Angela March Day. A birth certificate and a death certificate. Her mother's whole life, crammed into one little crate.

Penelope could barely see through the tears, but when she hugged her father, she could feel his wet face against hers. Overwhelmed, she lay down in her hammock.

Her father wiped his face and plucked a picture from the crate. It was a washed-out snapshot of Penelope's mother, young and beautiful, head thrown back in laughter, holding a baby girl on her hip while trying to play Ping-Pong. Then he pulled the blanket up to Penelope's chin and said, "Let me tell you a story."

ACKNOWLEDGMENTS

Like every writer, I've got my people—the ones who did the heavy lifting of real life while I was writing—and I owe them endless thanks. That means Wendy Loggia, an editor of unlimited grace and enthusiasm; Matthew Elblonk, who saw potential where others saw junk mail; Alexandria Neonakis and Katrina Damkoehler, who brought their twisted magic to the striking cover; and Carrie Andrews for the copyediting heroics. But gratitude also goes to Kenn and Julie, David and Devora, and Ben and Ursina for infinite kindness and devotion; Jon Eig, Mark Caro, Jim Garner, and the rest of the Hunger Dungers for their beautiful brains and beers; Brad Sweeney and Anne-Marie Guarnieri for their hospitality; Jeff Johns and Diana Bump for the porch with a birdhouse view; Dan Saxe for the air mattress in Brooklyn; Jason Saldanha for making the connection; Robert Baker for unlocking the door; Fang Island for the godlike noise; and Penny Pollack for taking a zillion chances on me. Hearty cheers to Charlotte Ostrow, Jocelyn, and Lee Ann, who picked up the eternal slack; CD Collins and Camilla and John Mendenhall, who provided sanctuary; and Joy Tutela, Melissa Walker, Beth Davey, Katie Alender, and Renee Zuckerbrot, who lent smart guidance. To Bud Ruby, Helene Catz, Eva Mumm, Philip Fox, and Mary Ann and Isaac Abella, whose blessed memories stir up color and sound. Special love to Hannah, who read it first and best; Max, who always demands a bedtime story; and Avi, who melts me every day; to Mom and Dad, who have always believed—and, of course, to Sarah, who never stops offering her hand and heart.

ABOUT THE AUTHOR

Jeffrey Michael Ruby is the chief dining critic of *Chicago* magazine. He is the coauthor of *Everybody Loves Pizza: The Deep Dish on America's Favorite Food* and has played college basketball in Ireland, assisted in an autopsy, and sumo wrestled for twenty thousand people in New Jersey. He lives in Chicago with his wife and three children. *Penelope March Is Melting* is his first work of fiction.